END OF THE LINE

EXPLORING BRITAIN'S RURAL RAILWAYS

END OF THE LINE

EXPLORING BRITAIN'S RURAL RAILWAYS

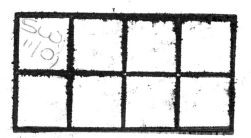

PAUL ATTERBURY

BOXTREE

First published in Great Britain in 1994 by Boxtree Limited, Broadwall House, 21 Broadwall, London SE1 9PL

10 9 8 7 6 5 4 3 2 1

ISBN 1 85283 538 9

Designed and conceived by Julian Holland Publishing Ltd
Edited by Sue Gordon
Cartography by Gecko Ltd
Picture research by Julian Holland

Printed and bound in Portugal by Printer Portuguesa

A CIP catalogue entry for this book is available from the British Library

The author would like to thank Sue Whitaker for making sense of his manuscript and would like to give special thanks to Caroline de Lane Lea for her support during the writing of this book. Finally, special thanks are due to British Rail, for the quality of their service and the courtesy of their staff on lines that are destined for ever to be 'unprofitable'

Photographic acknowledgements
All photography by Roy Chapman except for the following:
Whitby Archives Heritage Centre: p11; The Francis Frith Collection: p12, p91b, p93, p97t, p133, p144; National Railway Museum: p17b, p20t, p57, p122b, p125; R.C. Riley: p24/25, p28, p29b, p33, p37, p44, p48, p90, p94, p97b, p99, p100t, p102, p103b, p105, p115t, p134, p135; Suffolk County Council Libraries & Heritage: p27, p32, p34, p35b; R.H. Tunstall: p38/39, p43; Dorset Natural History & Archeological Society: p41, p47; Dorset County Council Libraries: p45b; Brian Morrison: p55; The National Library of Wales: p65, p66, p120, p131; The Sankey Collection: p73, p75, p80, p81b, p84; Julian Holland: p81t, p110; Paul Atterbury: p71; Peter Berry: p74, p85; Cornwall County Council: p89, p95b; S.C. Nash: p106, p108, p111, p113; Gwynedd County Council: p143; The Wick Society: p157, p158, p159, p160; Whyte Photographic Archive: p149, p153
Author photo by Caroline De Lane Lea

Contents

Introduction

'The railways are dreadful . . . Today I have come an immense distance, about 200 miles, continually changing carriages & lines.' These are typical comments from the 1851 diary of the famous Victorian architect and designer, Augustus Welby Northmore Pugin who, although dependent upon the burgeoning railway network in Britain was, like many of his contemporaries, no lover of trains. There are many references to delays caused by poor connections, inefficiency and inadequate services, and to the practical difficulties and inconveniences that were the inevitable results of a fragmented but often expensive system of independent and often localised companies.

The whole pattern of railway development through the 19th century, in Britain and elsewhere, was a steady progression towards the creation of a large network operated by a small number of major companies, able to handle the complexities of a truly national railway. The experience of the First World War proved once and for all that small companies simply could not cope, either operationally or financially, with the demands of a national network, and this resulted in the 1923 groupings that formed the big four, the Great Western, the Southern, the London, Midland & Scottish and the London & North Eastern. In the 1930s the big four, backed by continued investment and financial success, were notable for their record of achievement, quality of service and social concern. However, even they were stretched to the limits by the Second World War, and the creation of the nationalised British Railways in 1948 was the next logical step, as much for practical as for political reasons.

British Railways, who inherited a network whose labyrinthine operating techniques and huge mileage reflected decades of private ownership, found the railways' traditional traffic steadily eroded by increasing government support for roads. By the late 1950s something had to be done and Dr Beeching was brought in to impose order on a chaotic system. His rationalisation programme, carried out through the 1960s and into the early 1970s, was draconian, depriving many parts of Britain of any kind of railway service. The rural lines bore the brunt of the cuts, with social needs increasingly buried beneath government-sponsored emphasis on profits. At the same time, the whole cost structure of transport remained heavily weighted towards roads. Despite this, British Railways continued to operate a genuinely national service that maintained a balance between main lines and the surviving rural routes in the face of constantly reducing government support.

For doctrinaire political reasons that have little to do with the needs of a national network, British Rail is being sacrificed on the altar of privatisation. At a time when, on a global scale, railways are increasingly seen as the only viable land-based transport system, the British network is to be fragmented and regionalised in order that money may be made from the sale of the profitable sectors. The direct result of this has to be the reduction of

Below *The old-style diesel multiple units still clung to life in July 1993 on the Liskeard to Looe branch line. A Looe-bound train runs alongside the East Looe river between Sandplace and Looe*

services and ultimately the loss of those lines that, though socially vital, can never hope to be independently profitable. It is easy, on a map of the network, to identify the lines that are now under threat and to see that, if current policies are maintained, large of areas of Britain will be deprived of the most practical form of public transport at a time when the whole emphasis on roads is being forced by international and environmental pressure into reverse.

This book is a record of journeys on rural railways throughout Britain, an exploration of some of the lines that may soon disappear. Included are West Country branch lines, the last survivors of their type, long cross-country routes in Wessex, Wales, East Anglia and Scotland, and journeys round the coast of Cumbria and along the valley of the Esk. A common theme is the sea, with all the lines starting or finishing on the coast. It is a book

about history and landscape, linking the past with the reality of the present, about people, and above all else about the last days of British Rail as a truly national network, before the enforced return to the fragmented, expensive and socially unbalanced system that Pugin knew so well.

Above *With Cader Idris in the background a Machynlleth to Pwllheli train slowly crosses the 113 span timber trestle viaduct across the Mawddach estuary at Barmouth in September 1993*

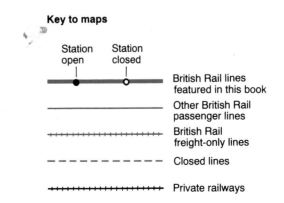

Key to maps

	Station open	Station closed	
●———○			British Rail lines featured in this book
———————			Other British Rail passenger lines
+++++++++++			British Rail freight-only lines
– – – – – –			Closed lines
++++++++++++			Private railways

The Esk Valley Line
Whitby to Middlesbrough

I T IS A SUNNY morning in Whitby. The train waits at the platform, its engines gently clattering. With their faded local colour scheme, a kind of cream with horizontal colour banding, the four coaches look a bit like a line of single-decker buses. The last couple of passengers wander along and then the driver, fair and in his twenties, finishes his chat with the guard, walks to the front of the train, unlocks his compartment, arranges his kitbag, his thermos and his paper and settles down, finally closing the door that hides him from view. Trains on quiet rural lines are often driven by elderly men on their way to retirement, slowing down after years at the demanding controls of InterCity expresses or long-distance freights, so the driver's age came as something of a surprise. Presumably the days when every small boy wanted to be an engine driver are long gone, but a job that is regular, reliable and varied clearly has plenty of appeal in an area of high unemployment, even if shuttling to and fro along the quiet lines of the Northeast might seem tame to someone who longs to hurtle down the East Coast main line at over a hundred miles an hour. The doors close, the guard buzzes twice, the driver's buzzer echoes in reply, the engines growl and the train creeps forward, gathering speed as it leaves the station. That day there were seven passengers and three British Rail men on the 08.55 from Whitby to Middlesbrough.

Scattered through the first three coaches, the passengers chatted, read their papers and only occasionally looked out at the view that was obviously very familiar. The guard moved among them, selling tickets and gossiping. The day return to Middlesbrough cost £7.50, high enough to deter casual use, and not nearly high enough to make the line cost effective in the harsh realities of a market

A Whitby to Middlesbrough train pauses at Danby to let off two young passengers

The Esk Valley Line
Whitby to Middlesbrough 35 miles

History of the line

In 1836 a horse-drawn passenger railway was opened between Whitby and Pickering, an isolated and old-fashioned line built entirely to satisfy local needs. With its leisurely methods of operation in what was already the steam age, and its complicated rope-hauled inclined plane, the railway went its own way until 1845, when it was taken over by the York & North Midland, the backbone of George Hudson's empire. Rapidly rebuilt and enlarged for steam operation, the old Whitby & Pickering soon lost its isolation, becoming the centre of a burgeoning local network. Hudson was very keen to develop the tourist potential of the Yorkshire Moors and the Yorkshire coast, and so Whitby was gradually linked to York and the Midlands, Middlesbrough and the North, and ultimately to Scarborough, and the rest of the coast. The railway network thus developed played a crucial role in building up both tourist and freight traffic, and the region continued to flourish until the Second World War. By that time, it was all part of the LNER, which had in turn taken over from the North Eastern Railway, the company that had absorbed all the local lines in the late nineteenth century. Declining traffic in the post-war period resulted in a gradual reduction of the network, and many of Whitby's links disappeared, including its original route south to Pickering. Today, as a result, Whitby is very much the end of the line.

Above *The bright colours of a Class 142 diesel as it waits for passengers at the truncated Battersby Junction*

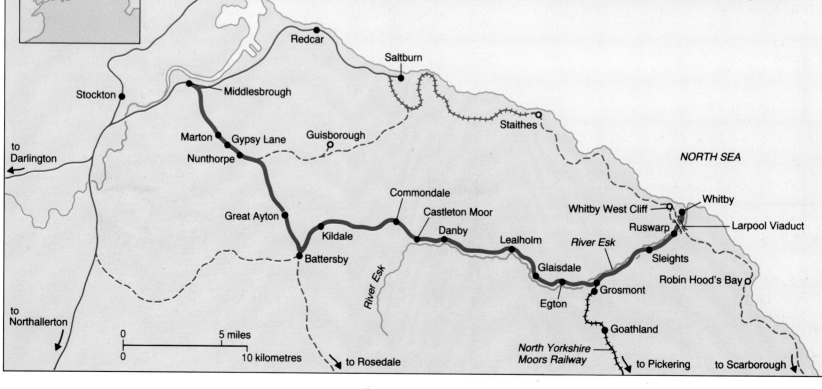

economy. Even when adequately supported, this line apparently cost ten times its actual income per passenger to run. On a bad day, in passenger terms, the money just drains away.

The Whitby line is the classic example of the problems faced by rural railways today. It has a glorious past that goes back to the dawn of passenger railways in Britain, it played a vital role through the nineteenth and early twentieth centuries in developing both industry and tourism in North Yorkshire, it was, with its connecting network, the backbone of social life in the region, and it has a delightful route along the Esk Valley – a landscape that is in every way as exciting as that of its very successful preserved steam-powered neighbour, the North Yorkshire Moors Railway. Despite all this, and despite the sympathetic support and the financial aid the line receives from local government, British Rail and the local tourist industry, the trains simply do not carry enough people. The hourly bus service is cheaper and quicker, but the routes do not include the Esk Valley and its villages. The Whitby line has always served an area of minor, winding roads, remote villages and isolated farms, and the people living in this valley have been dependent on the trains for over a hundred and fifty years. Where car ownership is by no means universal, the railway is a lifeline and if it were to disappear it would have to be replaced by a complex structure of community buses and care car services. Keeping the trains must be a more sensible option, even when they are under-used.

From October to May, four trains run to and fro, Monday to Saturday, between Whitby and Middlesbrough. The perversely unhelpful timetable means there is no early morning service to Middlesbrough, so the trains cannot be used by people going to work or to school, while those wanting to visit Whitby for the day from Middlesbrough have either to catch a train at a time most tourists are still asleep, or have only half a day in the town. There are no trains on Sunday,

Right *Viewed from the harbour, an LNER locomotive stands on the turntable near Whitby station in 1937*

Above *A wonderful view of the approaches to Whitby station, the Abbey and the river Esk, taken from Larpool in 1886. The line on the left climbs up to Whitby West Cliff, while the lower is the line to Grosmont*

although this is presumably a popular day for visits to Whitby and the North Yorkshire Moors Railway, and evening travel is out of the question. In practical terms, therefore, for the greater part of the year the Whitby line is useful only for shopping, for the retired and the unemployed, and for tourists prepared to tolerate the eccentricities of the timetable. A few years ago there were eight trains each way and four on Sundays, and early morning trains on weekdays in both directions. The summer timetable is, admittedly, better, and includes a Sunday service aimed at the needs of tourism. However, the essential needs of the local community are not seasonal, and it is increasingly

these that rural railways are being compelled, by the policies of centralised government, to ignore. What is disappearing fast is that fundamental belief upon which the British railway network was built, namely that everyone has a right to accessible public transport. Once this has been thoroughly undermined, the real reason for running a rural railway has gone. On their own, the other reasons, historical, emotional or whatever, simply do not stand up. There is no doubt that British Rail does its best under a government that shows a shameful and irresponsible lack of interest, but it is hard to draw a distinction between necessary economies and that old trick of closing a railway by running services at times no one wants them.

In the current political climate, where short-term thinking rules the roost, the Whitby line, and all the others like it in Britain, must be doomed. What private company would even consider taking on a line that is never likely to cover its costs, let alone make a profit? The great white hope for railways such as the Whitby line is tourism, but is it right that routes whose social importance is considerable, and whose economic potential is unrealised, have no future other than as linear theme parks? The success of the preserved railway movement has been remarkable, and further growth is likely to be encouraged by the reduction of the national rail network to a series of high-cost InterCity routes. With its beautiful Esk Valley route, the Whitby line, or at least the section from Grosmont to Whitby, must be seen as a prime candidate for this treatment. However, even allowing for the hidden subsidy of low-cost or free enthusiast labour, there is surely a limit to the number of such lines that the tourist industry can support.

The Whitby line also highlights a legacy of the Beeching era that is often overlooked. Many of the lines that appeared to survive that period of drastic rationalisation were actually doomed instead to a slow and lingering death. At Whitby, as in so many other places, Beeching destroyed the core of a local network, and the bits that remained were fragmented and detached from any practical economic viability. Beeching wanted to close the Whitby line, but local pressure kept it open. He may have lost that particular battle, but he must have known that he had won the war. Isolated and cut off from its economic roots, the Whitby line even then can have had a very uncertain future.

The railway history of the north Yorkshire coast is unusually interesting. It starts in 1836, with the opening of the horse-drawn passenger railway between Whitby and Pickering. Engineered by George Stephenson, and built with a rope-hauled inclined plane incorporated in its route, this line pioneered the principle of railway travel in what was then a very isolated region. Nine years later the line was bought by the York & North Midland Railway and merged into the burgeoning railway

empire being developed by the tycoon George Hudson, then at the height of his powers. It was the York & North Midland that inspired the rapid industrial growth of north Yorkshire during the second quarter of the nineteenth century, using the existing foundation of traditional industries such as ship building, engineering and coal. Railways were, in any case, well established in this region, following the success of the Stockton & Darlington from 1825, and an extensive network was soon created to serve the Tees and its surrounding centres of industry. While freight traffic was the driving force behind Hudson's empire, he was well aware of the potential for passenger carrying in an area whose physical qualities made inevitable a great expansion in tourism. Although Scarborough had been a popular spa since the seventeenth century, it was Hudson who really turned it into a major resort by making it readily accessible by train. It was his railways that made popular the Yorkshire coast and revealed for the first time to a

Below A solitary passenger awaits the arrival of the approaching train to Middlesbrough at Sleights station

Above *The classic façade of Whitby station with indications of its current use as an Indian restaurant*

George Hudson

Popularly known as the Railway King, George Hudson started life as a draper in York. A successful speculation in railway shares led to many more, and during the heady 1840s, when Britain was gripped by railway mania, he quickly built up a huge personal fortune. His power base was the Northeast of England, and he soon controlled the major companies of the region, the York & North Midland, and the Newcastle & Berwick. Upon these and other companies he created an immense empire, with tentacles spreading northwards to Scotland, southwards to the Midlands and all over the Northwest. By 1846 he controlled nearly half of Britain's railways, had risen to be Lord Mayor of York, MP for Sunderland and the first railway millionaire in Britain. His empire was built on speculation, corporate manipulation, shrewd management and luck but, like many financiers before and since, he knew little about how his business actually operated. An aggressive and argumentative man, he had many enemies and in the competitive atmosphere of the times, it was soon apparent that not all his deals were as clean as they might have been. Overstretched and running out of both credit and friends, he was forced to flee the country in 1855, his empire and his fortune in ruins.

broad market the particular qualities of the landscape of the Yorkshire moorlands, the Cleveland hills and the river valleys of the Dales.

In the 1840s the Whitby to Pickering line was rebuilt to be suitable for steam haulage and at the same time Whitby's grand new classical-style station became the centre of an expanding network of local lines, developed over the next forty years. Railways wound their way along the coast to north and to south, linking Scarborough with Middlesbrough, and opening up to tourism places such as Robin Hood's Bay, which had hitherto been virtually inaccessible other than by boat. At the Pickering end, the line was extended southwards, giving trains from York, and thus from other parts of the north and the Midlands, direct access to Whitby and the coast. From Grosmont a new line was driven westwards, opening up a quicker inland route to Middlesbrough, Stockton and the Northeast. Development continued through the nineteenth century, and stations and other facilities were steadily enlarged to cope with the great boom in tourism that characterised the last decades of Victoria's reign. Freight was also important, with cargoes as diverse as stone, coal, iron products and fish adding their weight to the railway company's revenues. This pattern continued well into the twentieth century as all the local companies were merged together, first into the North Eastern Railway, and then in 1923 into the great LNER whose network covered the east of Britain, from London and Essex to the north of Scotland. Whitby remained a busy centre of its local network until the closures of the 1960s which swept much of it away. Among the lines to disappear were the coastal route from Scarborough to Saltburn and the connecting cross-country Guisborough link, the route south from Grosmont to Pickering and beyond, and the direct route to Stockton and the Northeast via Battersby. The only line to survive was the Middlesbrough to Whitby, but a glance at a map makes it clear that this route was never going to be viable on its own. Deprived of its network of connecting tourist, passenger and freight lines, the railway to Whitby alone did not make much sense, except as a social necessity. In the post-Beeching era, there was a policy that enabled loss-making lines of local importance to be carried by the major revenue earning routes. However, more recent policy has been to expect all lines to be self-supporting or to be operated with subsidies paid by local government and other non-railway bodies, and under those rules the Whitby line has become increasingly a liability with little chance of paying its way. British Rail has done all it can to reduce operating costs and has reached a point where no further savings can be made without stopping the trains altogether. During the last ten years extensive marketing campaigns have promoted the line as one of Britain's scenic railways, with posters, special leaflets and links with the other tourist attractions of Whitby and its region, along with colourful line guides. There has even been a special video on the line, introduced by Geoffrey Smith, the TV gardening expert, and sold by British Rail at £9.95.

Another source of revenue was the reopening, in 1973, by the North Yorkshire Moors Railway, of the line from Grosmont to Pickering, and its subsequent operation as a steam tourist route. This is now one of the premier preserved railways in Britain, thanks largely to the dramatic quality of its landscape, but for much of the year it is unable to benefit from its direct link with the main British Rail network because of the inadequacies of the Middlesbrough–Whitby timetable.

Whitby station is an imposing building, in the heart of the town and right by the port. It was designed by George Townsend Andrews, a close friend of George Hudson and the architect, as a result, of many of the stations in the area, including Hull and Scarborough. Its elegant stone classicism was originally graced by a hipped roof over the train shed, but this has long disappeared. Still present, however, is the porte-cochère with its arched arcade, and a decorative tiled map of the North Eastern Railway network, made by Craven Dunnill of Shropshire early this century. Another one survives at Middlesbrough, mute testimony to all those lines that have gone. The maps also preserve some of the extraordinary names carried by stations long extinct in the region, Potto,

Above *Ex-WD locomotive,* Dame Vera Lynn, *with admirers, young and old, at Grosmont station, North Yorkshire Moors Railway*

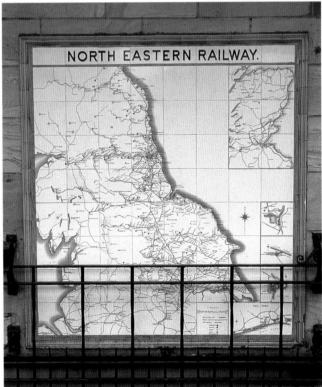

Left *The decorative tiled map of the North Eastern Railway still survives at Whitby station*

Sexhow, Yarm, Grinkle, Fighting Cocks and Boosbeck. Perhaps the enamel plaques that carried such names live on in some railway museum or enthusiast's front parlour. The station is a proper terminus on a small scale, and the few trains that come do still wait roughly where they should, within the area once spanned by the train shed roof. The only problem is that, apart from the building itself and its tangible history, it is not really a station in the usual meaning of the term. Its rooms house an Indian restaurant, a tea shop, a gallery and other interesting diversions but there is nowhere to buy a ticket, or do any of those other things usually associated with train travel.

Having overcome these problems, encountered now all too often in provincial stations, by simply getting into the waiting train, the journey proper begins. As it leaves the station the train is immediately beside the Esk, with a wonderful view of boats and all the usual colourful paraphernalia of a port set against the background of the town and its harbour. At its heart is the old bridge and, high on the hills above, the ruins of the abbey look down over what is still one of Britain's most delightful seaports, one whose long history and compact streets have survived the usual excesses of the tourism industry. Dracula, kippers, Captain Cook, jet jewellery and the odd whale make unusual bedfellows, but somehow Whitby manages to make the most of this complex pattern of historical legacy, and still remains a charming place.

The line runs along the bank of the Esk, passing old boatyards and mouldering wrecks while the waters sparkle in the sun as they run towards the sea. The massive Larpool viaduct comes into view, a series of tall but delicate brick arches built in 1885 to carry high over the Esk the line from Scarborough to Whitby. Long disused, the viaduct's thirteen arches, reputed to contain five million bricks, stand as a reminder of complicated railway practices. Trains from Scarborough and the south would cross the viaduct and continue to a station

Left *The massive Larpool Viaduct which used to carry the Scarborough to Saltburn line across the river Esk*

Left *Ruswarp station, first stop out of Whitby*

Below *Grosmont Junction, seen in North Eastern Railway days. The line to the left is for Pickering, the line to the right is for Battersby Junction and Middlesbrough*

high above Whitby called West Cliff. They would then reverse down a steep and sharply curved horseshoe-shaped track into Whitby station, passing under the viaduct on the way. Trains going north from Whitby along the coastal route would have set off in the same manner.

The first stop is Ruswarp and here is the first, and one of the best preserved, of the characteristic stone-built stations, all chunky rustication and stepped gables. This one still boasts its clock, set firmly into the stonework. It does not seem to go but at least it is still there. Most of the other stations just have a round hole where the clock used to be. One person got on at Ruswarp, falling immediately into conversation with somebody already on the train. It is that kind of journey. The train twists and turns along the river valley, the wheels screaming on the curves and bumping along the track in a way that indicates its minimal maintenance status. The surroundings are the river, still wide and fast-flowing between wooded banks, and that vision of backyard England that is always one of the pleasures of a rural railway journey. Gardens obsessively neat stand side by side with unkempt and uncared for muddles of weeds and domestic clutter. An abandoned Reliant shares its field with some horses and the inevitable black plastic bales. Surprisingly, the Esk is an important salmon river, and at Sleights the fish leap over the rocks on their way upstream. The grey stone village is set back on

the hillside, and one more person had wandered down to catch the train. A big steel bridge carries the main road across the track and the river, while a separate footbridge leads to the village. On the station, and on most stations on the line, is a colourful board pointing out local features of interest and suggesting walks in the area. These were installed in the late 1980s, when there was the last serious attempt at developing the line's tourist potential. From Sleights the line criss-crosses the Esk. There are no less than twelve river crossings in the nine miles between Whitby and Glaisdale, many of which would have been built for the original Whitby to Pickering route, an expensive undertaking on an essentially local line. The river now rushes between rocky and wooded banks, their steep sides enriched by the occasional waterfall, and then it all opens out as the moors appear. At Grosmont the station is preceded by the

Right *A Whitby-bound train departs from Egton station*

Above *Instructions to stop at Glaisdale station*

unexpected sight of sidings, lines of maroon-coloured carriages in various states of repair, and the selection of arcane and antiquated bits and pieces that mark the province of every preserved railway. The station is Y-shaped, with the main buildings flanking the original line to Pickering, now the North Yorkshire Moors Railway, while the British Rail line branches away to the right, its passengers having to put up with a sort of shed backing on to a windy car park. A couple of elderly but fit-looking men got off, obviously on their way to a day bashing bits of old metal, or polishing ancient paintwork in the NYMR workshops.

Egton is famous for its annual gooseberry show, but little else in the quiet village that surrounds the large Norman-style Victorian church. Two more passengers got on here, and then the train rattled on to Glaisdale. It sat in the station for a while. Passengers chatted, and the station geese kept up a banter of annoyed honking while the exchange of tokens took place. The token is a well-known feature of single-track life, and its simplicity goes back to the earliest days of railway operation. To ensure safe operation of single-tracked routes with trains in both directions, the line was divided into sections, each in the care of a signalman. He could not allow a train to enter his section until he had issued it with the token, usually a leather bag attached to a large metal hoop. If he did not have the token, the train would wait in a passing loop until the one coming from the other direction arrived with it and it could then be returned and given to the waiting train. Tokens, therefore, spent their time being carried to and fro in the cabs of locomotives, and the exchange of the token gave the driver and the signalman a good opportunity to catch up on local gossip. The token system is still widely used on British Rail's single-tracked goods and passenger lines, but economies have often removed the signalman, and made the whole business more solitary. A few years ago, when the signal box at Glaisdale, along with others on the line, was still in use, the token would be given to the driver by the signalman or, as was often the case here, tossed across the track in a rather dashing manner. All that has now gone, replaced by two metal cupboards on the platform, one labelled

Whitby to Glaisdale, the other Glaisdale to Battersby. The driver opens them up, replaces the token for the section now passed, and takes the token for the next section. He stands in the sun chatting on the telephone that lurks in the cupboard, presumably to the line's controller, and then locks up again, climbs back into his cab and the train sets off. It is a wonderfully old-fashioned process and, on this line, almost unnecessary in the winter as the chances of meeting another train must be negligible as there is only one train going to and fro. In case the driver does forget, a big sign tells him to Stop Obtain Token and Permission to Proceed. Railway signs are often satisfyingly correct and old-fashioned in their use of language, even modern ones like this, and refreshing after the abrupt illiteracy of so many road signs. Alternatively, they are in a kind of private code that makes them impenetrable to outsiders. Once worked out, SW ('short whistle') is fairly clear-cut, but messages such as 'Shunting Bell' and 'When Flashing Telephone' are open to all sorts of interpretations. Glaisdale was once a centre of the iron industry, with three blast furnaces, but all that is long gone. Now it is more famous for the stone bridge over the Esk, built in 1619, and known as the Beggar's Bridge to commemorate a romantic tale about a local lad who fell in love with the squire's daughter, was rebuffed, went away to make his fortune and came back to marry her, and build the

Above *New use for a station: Bed and breakfast at Glaisdale*

Left *The latest technology - the electronic token boxes at Glaisdale station which have recently made the signalman's job a thing of the past*

bridge. It is certainly a handsome bridge, and it seems to have influenced many of those along the line, markedly fine in the quality of their stonework.

The distinctive Esk Valley landscape continues to Lealholm, a surprisingly large station in the middle of nowhere, with an old goods shed and other echoes of a time when railways really served their communities. No one got on or off, and the train went on through a broadening landscape to Danby, known as the 'village of the Danes', and well placed for the North York Moors National Park. Danby's classic stone-built station is now, like all the others on this line, nothing to do with the railway. As the train waits, passengers have intimate views of the private lives these buildings contain, with ample time to study the wallpapers and the ornaments.

The line now crosses moorland with distant views of hills, a landscape of heather and bracken, stone walls and isolated farms. At Castleton Moor three people appear out of nowhere to catch the train, and by now there are enough passengers to establish a pattern, mostly elderly, and more women than men. It was here too that a woman left the train, carrying her shopping bags, and walked

away from the platform straight into the empty fields, to disappear slowly up a well-defined path. For her, the train was a vital part of a weekly routine, and for her, and the many like her living along the route, its continued existence is a social necessity, not an act of charity. Commondale is little more than a halt and then it is on to Kildale, at the heart of the moors, and with the Cleveland Hills looming on the horizon. Here is a particular vision of English life, a terrace of stone cottages, basic but elegant, a chapel, and nothing else on an ocean of empty moorland. After Kildale the train moves into a different landscape of big hills, with ever more dominant the 1,000ft peak of Roseberry Topping.

Battersby Junction was once the place where the main line to Stockton and the Northeast met the line to Middlesbrough. A branch line from this once-busy junction also once ran south and east into the Cleveland Hills to the iron-ore mines at Rosedale. With everything south and west of Battersby long gone, the train has to make sense of the fragments that remain. This means it comes into what is now a dead end, a curious collection of huts marked by a fine 1907 North Eastern Railway water column, it waits while the driver goes through the

Above *Castleton station in North Eastern Railway days*

Left *Trespassing geese cross the line at Commondale*

Right *A mixed train of Sprinter and Class 142 diesels pauses at Commondale station while hikers head for the hills*

token ceremony again, and it then sets off back the way it has just come for a short distance before branching away to the left.

The next stop is Great Ayton, a village straddling the banks of the river Leven and famous for its Captain Cook associations. The old school he attended is now a museum, while the Cook Monument is the obelisk high on a nearby hill that is visible for miles from the train. Minor roads cross the track, sometimes with only lights and sound signals to warn traffic of an approaching train. It is curious that the international road signal for an ungated level crossing is still a steam locomotive. There must be many drivers who have never seen such a thing. At Nunthorpe there is an even more archaic survival, a level crossing whose gates are still operated by a signalman turning a great wheel high in his box. It is here that the moorland landscape is left behind, replaced by more domestic surroundings, bungalows and a bowling club, gardens and garden sheds, and the intimacy of back lawns and washing lines. Gypsy Lane is that rare commodity, a relatively new station built to serve the spreading suburbia of Middlesbrough. Estates of boxy houses spread in all directions. Five very smart ladies got on here, clothes and hair all set for a shopping expedition to town, along with an incongruous figure, a man wearing a cloth cap and a muffler. Marton is another suburban station, with a golf course nearby, and then Middlesbrough begins to take over, first with its industrial estates and shopping centres, and then with its older industrial centre. The train moves towards an exciting skyline of cranes, clocktowers, refinery tanks, tower blocks and Victorian spires. The focal point is the transporter bridge, its delicate girders set high above the Tees. The journey ends amid the splendour of Middlesbrough's once great station. Gone is the dramatic lancet-shaped iron train shed, the victim of Second World War bombing, but plenty of decorative ironwork remains, along with the splendid 1877 French Gothic style booking hall with its hammerbeam roof and decorative tiled frieze, recently restored and certainly one of Middlesbrough's better sights. Here is a kind of railway normality again, with trains to distant

places such as Newcastle and Leeds, along with more local ones serving that other fragment of the Whitby network, the coastal route to Redcar and Saltburn. Not long after it had arrived, the train set off back to Whitby carrying five people on a private tour of the Esk Valley, trying hard to maintain a service against the odds.

Opposite *A Middlesbrough-bound Sprinter crosses Wayworth Moor, between Commondale and Kildale*

Left *The beautifully preserved 1907 North Eastern Railway water column at Battersby Junction waits for its next ghostly customer*

Above *Old technology – LNER Annett's Patent Point Lock still in use at Battersby Junction*

The East Suffolk Line
Ipswich to Lowestoft

ANYONE TRAVELLING by train from Ipswich to Lowestoft has that rare luxury, a choice of routes. Most people, unaware that the choice exists, take the old Great Eastern line up to Norwich, now a relatively painless electrified modern route, and change there for Lowestoft. It is a journey of two football teams, from Portman Road to Carrow Road, from the blue and white of Ipswich Town to the yellow and green of Norwich City, teams with a reputation for style and elegance whose grounds are both within reach of the station.

Ipswich station is an unusual place, with plenty to catch the eye. Opened in 1860, it originally had one long platform, used by trains in both directions. This early nineteenth-century cost-saving eccentricity, once common, now survives in this part of Britain only at Cambridge. Ipswich station is an Italianate building in white local brick, a symmetrical design by Robert Sinclair with heavily pedimented wings flanking the central block. Adjacent to the southern end of its platforms is the mouth of the only tunnel in East Anglia. There is always plenty going on around the station, although traffic today is but a shadow of what it used to be. An old branch line, rarely, if ever, used, leads down to the docks which were once the core of the town's rail traffic. The growth of the container port at nearby Felixstowe may have brought about a steady decline in Ipswich's maritime life, but it has in turn engendered a new type of rail traffic. As a result, Ipswich still has a locomotive depot, and various elderly diesels in the strange freight liveries currently used by British Rail are generally to be seen resting in sidings near the platforms, waiting their turn to haul the container trains up and down the short Felixstowe branch.

Ex-LNER Class B17/6 4-6-0 No.61670 City of London, *with a Yarmouth to Liverpool Street train at Woodbridge on 10 October 1956*

The East Suffolk Line
Ipswich to Lowestoft 49 miles

History of the line

The Great Eastern Railway was formed in 1862 by an amalgamation of all the major East Anglia railways, notably the Eastern Counties, the Eastern Union and the Norfolk Railway, along with a number of smaller companies. Among these were the Stour Valley, the Ipswich & Bury and the grandly named Halesworth, Beccles & Hadiscoe Railway, the builders of much of what is now the East Suffolk line. The line was opened in part by 1854 and throughout, from Ipswich to Yarmouth and Lowestoft, in 1859 by the newly established East Suffolk Railway. It was operated, with its branches and connections, as an important secondary line by the Great Eastern through the nineteenth century.

The East Suffolk served both local needs and the seasonal demands of the new tourist traffic, the latter growing rapidly during the years after the First World War. Freight was also important, with the local harbours of Ipswich, Felixstowe, Snape, Aldeburgh, Southwold and, of course, Lowestoft, making the most of their rail connections. The major cargo was fish, but the trains also served local industry and agriculture. In 1923 the Great Eastern was, in turn, absorbed into the LNER, who continued to run the line until nationalisation. A steady decline in both passenger and freight traffic brought the first closures in the 1950s, to both stations and parts of the network, a process which continued into the Beeching era.

Left *Oulton Broad Swing Bridge signal box, 116 miles from Liverpool Street*

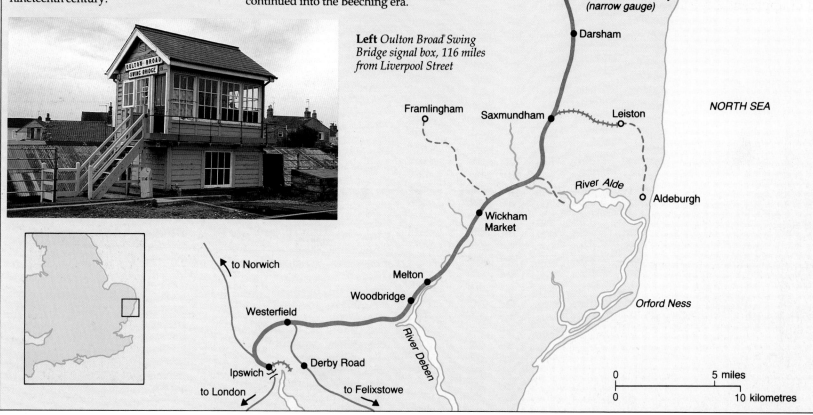

There are also rows of fuel oil wagons and, in more distant sidings, some old guard's vans, relics from a previous age of what were then called goods trains. Properly called brake vans, they were exactly that, heavy vehicles with brakes strong enough to stop a train of unbraked wagons from running away out of control. Now they wait, quietly decaying, to be called for occasional use on maintenance trains, to be sent away to be broken up, or, if they are very lucky, to be taken to embark on a new life in some preserved railway.

The InterCity expresses that pause briefly at Ipswich use the main platforms, their passengers probably oblivious of the various local services that depart from the bay platforms. From here there are trains to Cambridge and Bury St Edmunds, Ely, Felixstowe and, most importantly, to Lowestoft.

The East Suffolk line from Ipswich to Lowestoft is a curious survivor, representing as it does the kind of apparent duplication that Dr Beeching was so good at cutting out. As ever, the duplication was the result of rival Victorian railway companies battling over the same routes, in this case the Eastern Counties and the Eastern Union Railways. A number of promoters wanted to challenge the established dominance of the main Eastern Counties Norwich to London route, which ran inland via Diss, Stowmarket and Ipswich. Notable among these was the entrepeneur and railway tycoon, Sir Samuel Morton Peto, who saw the more direct coastal route to Lowestoft as a way to fulfil his ambitious plans for the development of that port. Like so many other lines, the East Suffolk was built in several parts. First there was the Halesworth, Beccles & Haddiscoe Railway, opened in 1854 to give these inland river towns direct access to Lowestoft and Norwich. Smaller companies such as the Yarmouth & Haddiscoe then extended it at both ends, and so by 1859 the Eastern Union and its associated companies had set up a

Below A classic pre-1911 view of Ipswich station with Great Eastern Railway trains waiting to leave on their journeys through East Anglia

Above *Ex-LNER Class K3 2-6-0 No.61973 departing from Lowestoft with a fish train on 9 October 1956*

its territory, rural and agricultural, but it also operated an enormous network of commuter services in and out of Liverpool Street, its London terminus, side by side with the lavishly equipped boat trains that linked with the Continental ferries at Harwich. Another, and very important, aspect of the company's activities was the fish trade from the East Coast ports. Indeed, Lowestoft as a port was essentially the creation of the Great Eastern, who from the 1860s developed a small local harbour into one of England's greatest fishing centres. In the absence of the heavy industry and coal mines from which many railway companies drew their major revenue, the Great Eastern had to make do with what it could find. The fish traffic was vital and it continued to be of importance into the days of the LNER, which absorbed the Great Eastern in 1923, and even into the post-nationalisation era of British Railways.

From the start of its Great Eastern days, the East Suffolk line became a secondary route, used primarily by passengers for short journeys along part of the route, a pattern that has basically never changed. There were through passenger and freight services from Yarmouth and Lowestoft to London, with expresses taking 150 minutes for the journey, but most trains were essentially local. At its peak in the nineteenth century there were rarely more than eight or ten trains daily in each direction, and the only real expansion occurred between the 1920s and the 1950s, largely due to increasing holiday traffic to East Coast resorts. There was even a holiday camp special to Gorleston on Sea on summer Saturdays in the 1950s. This traffic was, of course, seasonal, and winter services were always much reduced. It is ironic that today the service is at least as good as, if not better than, it was in the nineteenth century. Freight was always important, with the through-running fish and milk trains to London, as well as a wide variety of more local traffic, the line acting as a backbone to a number of branches and connecting routes, most of which had been set up to serve local harbours such as Snape, Aldeburgh, Southwold, and the Norfolk river ports.

Today, the freight traffic has largely gone, along with most of the branches and the connections, and

completely separate route from London to Yarmouth and Lowestoft, via Woodbridge, bringing together its various components under the name of the East Suffolk Railway. Shorter in miles, this was, however, always a more leisurely journey, establishing a pattern of operation that was the foundation for what remains today. The hoped-for expansion of trade and commerce in the region that was supposed to follow the railway's opening never really occurred. New industries were certainly established, notably milling, malting and agricultural engineering. Agriculture was itself important, with corn, flour and milk important cargoes, but in general there was little growth, with the populations of towns such as Woodbridge, Halesworth, Saxmundham and Beccles not altering significantly through the nineteenth century.

In 1862 all the railways of the region came under the control of the Great Eastern, and from that point onwards the former rival lines were run as part of a larger network.

The Great Eastern was a company of surprising diversity. Much of its traffic was, by the nature of

what remains is a classic rural railway, serving local needs. Its route is a tour of the gently undulating Suffolk landscape, a landscape with a quiet quality that will be familiar to those who enjoy East Anglian painters such as Cotman or Constable, a landscape of big fields broken by rivers, streams, hedges and copses, low horizons and huge skies, occasional villages marked by the tall stone towers of the churches. It is also a route notable for the large number of level crossings, many of which still have their original keeper's cottages, simple, traditional structures enhanced with decorative brickwork. Apart from its major buildings, the Great Eastern was generally a conservative company in architectural terms, but it did things with style, making the most of local materials and building types. A number of stations, for example Needham Market, have Flemish gables and other details characteristic of East Anglia, and similar elements can be found on parts of the Liverpool Street terminus in London. On the Lowestoft line there is nothing like this, but the buildings are not

Above *waiting for the train at Woodbridge*

Left *Ex-LNER Class D16 4-6-0 No.62546 departs from Halesworth with an Ipswich to Lowestoft train on 10 October 1956*

Opposite An Ipswich-bound train pauses at Woodbridge station, situated on the banks of the river Deben

without quality and their unity of style adds interest to the journey. This is a railway with a strongly regional character, in its landscape, in the towns and villages it serves, in its buildings and structures, and in the people who use it. It is exactly this quality of regionalism that will be swept away if the network is further reduced.

There is quite a good service on the Lowestoft line, and the trains are generally well used, despite their having no obvious tourist appeal. There are no sites of particular importance along the route, but there is plenty to see in towns like Woodbridge, Saxmundham and Beccles for those prepared to make an effort. Lowestoft, at the end of the line, is perhaps an acquired taste, but it has the enormous advantage of the sea, an essential ingredient of any good train journey in Britain. The route is a journey of East Anglian rivers, the Orwell, the Deben, the Alde and the Waveney, never far from the sea, but the landscape alone will not fill the trains with tourists.

Idling in an Ipswich bay platform, the 14.45 had no need of tourists. It was a single car, diesel Sprinter, and most of the seats were already filled before the connecting London train arrived. When it did, a flurry of people took those that remained, and the train then set off. Its passengers were a mixed bunch, some young, some old, some with children, obviously on the way home from a shopping trip, some smart, some not so. One lady was at work on her personal computer, and near her a gaggle of small boys played with a huge collection of toy cars and lorries, encouraged by their father while their mother looked away, studiously reading the small print on the back of her ticket. A group of girls, giggling, unruly, occasionally outrageous, discussed shopping, boys and other related topics. The elderly ticket collector moved among them, returning their banter, calling them by name, as they did in return. He seemed to know many of the passengers along the line and chatted to them all as they came and went.

The train ground its way past the freight sidings, across the main lines, and then branched right, crossing the Orwell, and quickly making its way past industry and suburbs to open country. A child marched up and down with a portable telephone that looked real, and rang periodically through the journey, but was a replica, a particularly annoying and teasing kind of toy to which only the child and her parents were oblivious. The first stop was Westerfield, once a rather grand station, with an old goods shed, a gabled structure with decorative cast iron details and, beneath the ivy that has almost enveloped it, attractively distressed paintwork in the old BR colours of cream and green. The building survives from the time of its original owners, the Felixstowe Railway & Pier Company, whose line to Felixstowe, which now branches away to the south, was opened in 1877. Felixstowe is one the few great successes of the local railways. The railway, and the port, were set up by a local landowner determined to build a rival to Harwich out of nothing, and his achievement in creating both a popular resort and a major docks complex laid the groundwork for what is still one of Britain's leading container terminals. In much better order

Below A single car Sprinter stands in the early morning sunlight at Ipswich station

Right *Ex-GER Class J15 0-6-0 No.65467, ambles through the Suffolk countryside with an Ipswich to Framlingham freight on 10 October 1956*

river is the site of the Sutton Hoo Anglo-Saxon ship burial. The single track, token-controlled section begins after Woodbridge, and the train crept along, beside the narrowing river, to Melton, a station closed in 1955 and then reopened for a new lease of life in 1984. Here, as at every station, a few people got off, and one or two got on, keeping the train fairly full. At a level crossing after Melton, there is one of those delightfully phrased railway notices, open to all kinds of interpretation, 'Wait for White Light and Whistle Before Proceeding.'

A landscape of open fields and narrow streams took the train to Wickham Market, a station actually in the village of Campsea Ashe, but named after another one two miles away. Here the smart ladies who had got on at Woodbridge elegantly descended. In the pre-Beeching era passengers changed here for the Framlingham branch, a slow

Above *A Victorian view of Woodbridge station, with a Great Eastern Railway train departing for Lowestoft*

Right *An Ipswich to Lowestoft single car Sprinter pauses at Halesworth station.*

than the goods shed is the signal box, still very much in use controlling the traffic on the busy branch, which curves round Ipswich and then follows the river Orwell to its estuary. At the next station, Bealings, the building is now a restaurant, its railway connections maintained by signs in BR Eastern region blue. The train climbed across the Suffolk hinterland and then dropped down gently towards the next river, the Deben. This is an exciting stretch, with the track running through a wide valley of mudflats, and boats of all kinds drawn up on the shore or neatly lined up in boatyards. At the centre of it all is Woodbridge station, a building with many original details, serving a town ranged up the hill away from the river and beneath the powerful church tower. Boats have always been important here. The Romans came up the Deben, and in the woods far across the

Ffestiniog. In fact now that the Trawsfynydd complex has been taken out of use, the latter's days may be numbered. Leiston was once famous for its ironworks and for Garratt's, a leading maker of steam road and agricultural engines. With fewer passengers, the ticket collector had more time to spend wandering from group to group, exchanging local gossip, while the children played with their toy lorries and the unruly girls chattered about the activities of the previous evening, their intimate revelations interspersed with raucous laughter. The next stop was Darsham, a remote station a long way from any village of significance. Surprisingly, a large group of passengers left the train here, more than at Saxmundham, and walked off purposefully down the lanes that seemed to lead to empty fields. Darsham too has a collection of original station buildings in good condition. As a whole, this line has been unusually lucky with its buildings, with few stations replaced by the bus shelter type of structure so common on other rural routes. Darsham is popular with visitors, being the most convenient station for walkers wishing to explore the Suffolk coast.

The landscape varies little, a pattern of gently undulating fields broken by patches of woodland, and scattered with old farms, whose attractive houses and outbuildings are marred, as ever, by that untidiness so characteristic of farmers. Old machinery is left rusting in exactly the spot where it

meander through the fields to the old market town behind a labouring locomotive that was close to retirement. Today, little remains of this, or of the branch to Snape, a goods line serving the little harbour at the head of the Alde Estuary. Right up to its closure in 1960, goods wagons at Snape were shunted by horses. There is another well-preserved group of buildings at Saxmundham station, including a goods shed and a signal box. The station itself still has its canopies. A number of people left the train, which now began to empty steadily at each succeeding station.

Soon after Saxmundham, the old branch to Aldeburgh swings away to the east. Passenger trains disappeared in the 1960s, but the tracks remain as far as Leiston, for the nuclear flask trains serving the Sizewell power station complex. It is an irony that at least three of Britain's threatened rural railways have been kept in commission, not to suit the needs of passengers, but because nuclear fuel flasks are the one cargo that not even the most anti-railway government will push on to the roads. The other two are the Cumbrian Coast line, serving Sellafield, and the Conwy Valley line to Blaenau

Above *The station building at Saxmundham now houses a restaurant and travel office*

Below *An Edwardian view of Saxmundham station circa 1911*

finally ceased working, piles of moulding black plastic straw bales dot the adjacent fields, and fine old barns slowly collapse back into the ground, while their modern replacements, great steel structures covered in corrugated tin, impose their vulgarity upon the countryside. The train crossed over the river Blyth and made its way into Halesworth, past old mills and maltings, with a distant view of the grand church, and then, surprisingly, past a busy textile factory. Through its big windows, right by the line and only a few feet from the passing train, there was a fine view of all the machinery rattling away, and the girls hard at work. East Anglia seems to specialise in these small, old-fashioned industrial towns, buried in the back of beyond, and yet surviving despite the odds. In the heartlands of the textile industry in the North, small mills such as this would have been driven out of business years ago, whereas in East Anglia a number of industries which have enjoyed a traditional stronghold for centuries are, remarkably, still there. Apart from textiles, the making of machinery and light engineering, this particular region is also famous for its printers, great names associated with Ipswich, Beccles and Bungay. Halesworth also has a good station, in this case enriched by delicately decorated cast iron detailing. Those with sharp eyes can see, just before the station, some brick pillars, one of the few visible remains of the Halesworth terminus of the old Southwold Railway, whose elderly trains ceased to amble along the beautiful Blyth Valley to the sea in the late 1920s. These pillars carried the footbridge that linked Southwold's station to the main line. The Blyth runs out to the sea between the delightful towns of Southwold and Walberswick, two old-fashioned resorts that have maintained their traditional East Coast quality, places still imbued with the light and colour captured in the late nineteenth-century paintings of Philip Wilson Steer. This is, in any case, a rich coastline, offering visitors nature reserves, bird sanctuaries, and the few remaining bits of medieval Dunwich that the sea has yet to swallow. It is merely a pity that the line was not built a few miles nearer the coast, for most of these places are difficult to reach by public

The Southwold Railway

Inspired by the town council's desire to put Southwold on the map and develop its tourist potential, the Southwold Railway Company was set up in 1876. Three years later its nine-mile route was opened, with intermediate stations at Wenhaston, Blythburgh and Walberswick. It was a single track, 3ft gauge line throughout, following the style of similar rural railways in France and Ireland. With its stock of three specially built locomotives and Continental-style carriages with open verandahs, the company operated a daily service of four trains each way, at a stately sixteen miles per hour. The line adequately fulfilled local needs, carrying at its peak over 100,000 passengers a year and a variety of freight, and was well supported by holidaymakers. Busy during the First World War and the early 1920s, the railway soon lost its way with the advent of connecting motor bus services, and the line closed for good in April 1929. Today, all that remains are the still discernible sections of the trackbed that offer gentle walks along the valley of the Blyth.

Below *The derelict narrow gauge Southwold Railway station at Halesworth in 1938, nine years after the closure of this line*

transport. Brampton is hardly a station at all, with not even a shed on its remote platform, and no one got on or off. It seems hard to believe that anyone ever does, there being nowhere to go to or come from. The survival of such minor stations represents the triumph of eccentricity over corporate logic.

Beccles is an attractive riverside town, but unfortunately few of its qualities are apparent from the train, or indeed from the station, a big place with many reminders of its former life as a major junction. Here was a railway crossroads, formed by the line from Ipswich and the south, which originally continued northwards to Yarmouth (with a complicated crossing of the Lowestoft to Norwich line at Haddiscoe), and an east–west route from Lowestoft to Beccles, Bungay, Harleston and Tivetshall, where it joined the main London to Norwich line. Today, all that remains is a half of each route, the other parts having been closed in the 1950s before Dr Beeching got to work. Trains from Ipswich therefore swing sharply to the right to

follow the low-lying marshlands of the river Waveney towards the sea. Now the landscape is a very different one, with the huge skies of the flat coastline filling the train's windows. The Waveney is below eye level, but in summer its route is marked by the cabin tops of the Broads holiday cruisers or the occasional sail apparently skimming across the fields.

Caravans announce the approach to Lowestoft, and the train stopped briefly at Oulton Broad South. From here a line used to run straight on to Lowestoft harbour and the docks station, but this disappeared long ago beneath a sprawl of holiday chalets. The train turned to the north, running past the harbour, with an exciting range of shipping views, and then crossed the swing bridge over Lake Lothing, an expanse of water linking the Broads and the Waveney to the sea at Lowestoft. In summer this is a colourful scene, with the waters to the west filled with holiday cruisers, while in winter the emphasis is on the fishing boats, the shipyards and the still busy docks. Leaving the

Below *An Ipswich-bound Sprinter crawls across the swing bridge at Oulton Broad shortly before arriving at Oulton Broad South station*

river, the train joined the Norwich line, with Oulton Broad North station tantalisingly out of reach just beyond the junction. It is an eccentric legacy of the Victorian railway builders that makes it impossible to travel by the same train between Oulton Broad North and Oulton Broad South.

Rattling along beside the docks and the huge empty sidings that used to handle the fish trains, the train crept into Lowestoft past a big old signal box, formerly the controlling heart of this once great complex. Lowestoft is a station haunted by echoes of days gone by, the ghosts of the freight trains that once filled the sidings, the ghosts of the holiday expresses that used to bring people in their thousands to the East Anglian resorts, and the ghosts of the trains that ran along the old coastal

line to Yarmouth. Today, little remains but the memories, and a much reduced station with a couple of platforms for the local trains from Norwich and Ipswich. It used to be called Lowestoft Central, but 'Central' has disappeared, along with Lowestoft's other stations. However, it is still in the heart of the town, with the sea no distance away. The few remaining passengers got off, disappearing quickly out of the station. The train paused briefly, just long enough for a crew changeover, and then set off again. Confusingly for those who had not read the timetable properly, it went not back to Ipswich, but on across the marshlands and alongside the river Yare to Norwich, from Portman Road to Carrow Road by the slow route.

Above *Diesel multiple units were already taking over steam duties when this photograph of Lowestoft engine shed was taken in October 1956*

Wessex Wanderings
Weymouth to Bristol

WEYMOUTH IS RARE among English coastal towns in having at its heart both a busy port and a magnificent sandy beach. First made popular by George III, whose surprisingly colourful statue decorates the esplanade, it has been a resort since the early nineteenth century. As ever, it was the coming of the railway, in Weymouth's case in the 1850s, that turned a local resort into a national holiday centre, and by the end of the century the town's station was the terminus for trains from as far afield as South Wales and Wolverhampton. With steamers sailing regularly from the port for the Channel Islands and for France, Weymouth was also, from quite an early date, the destination for special boat trains from London. A second station was built on the quay to serve these trains, connected to the main station by a line that wound its way through the middle of the town. Until a few years ago, when the service was withdrawn and the quay station closed, Weymouth was the only place in England where one could still come across a train creeping through streets crowded with pedestrians and cars. It was an entertaining and archaic sight, the train moving at a walking pace, preceded by men with flags and lamps, its sudden appearance causing consternation to motorists. In its heyday the quay station was a busy place, handling both passenger and freight trains, and as late as the 1960s trains making their way to the quay in the middle of the night to catch the overnight boats must have played havoc with the sleeping patterns of those who lived along the route. Today the tracks remain, but the only trains to visit the site of the once grand quay station are the very occasional charter specials. Those using the modern catamaran services to the Channel Islands have to get to the quay by other means.

Ex-GWR 0-6-0 pannier tank, No.9756, hauls an up Channel Island boat train through the streets of Weymouth on 10 July 1951

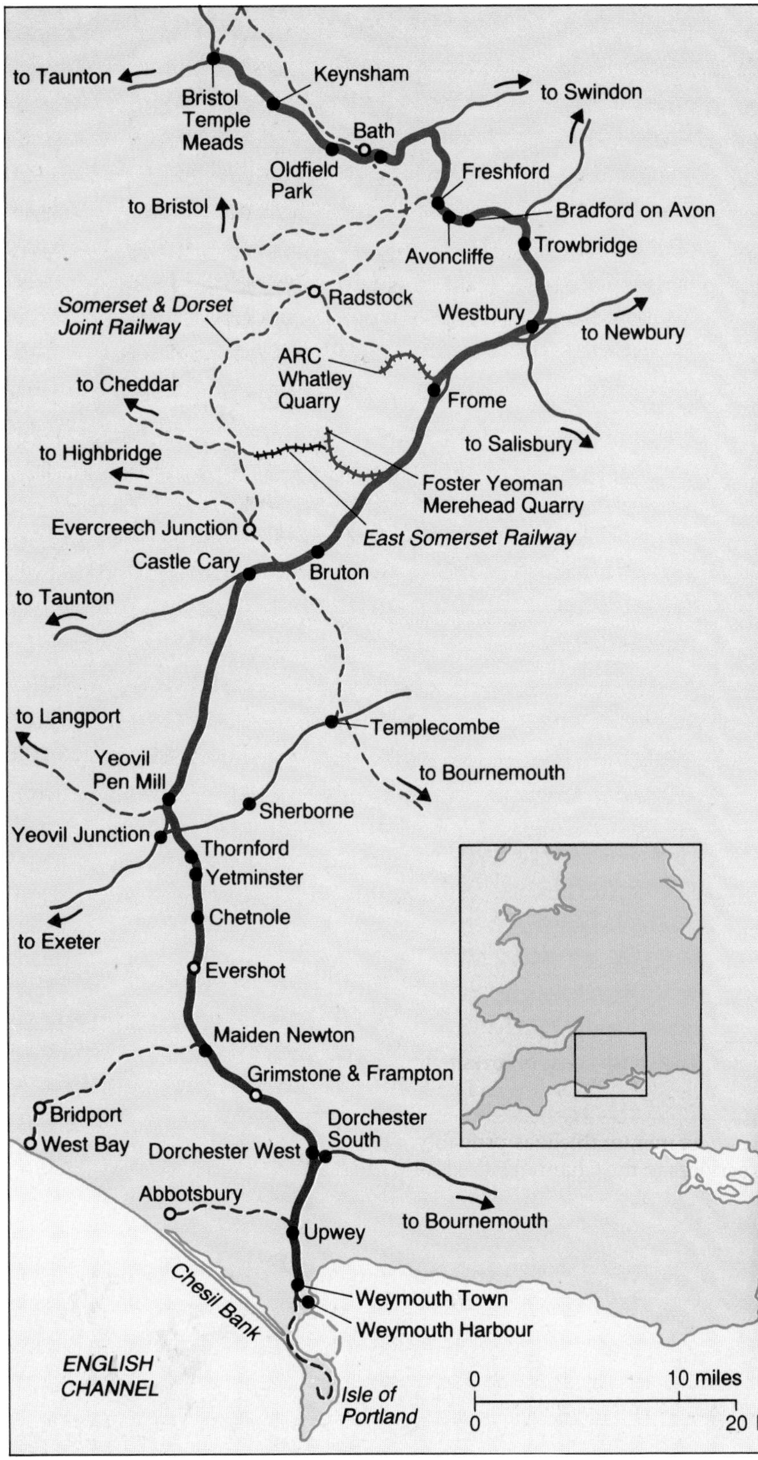

Map labels (left):

to Taunton ← Bristol Temple Meads
Keynsham
to Swindon →
Bath
Oldfield Park
Freshford
to Bristol ↑
Bradford on Avon
Avoncliffe
Trowbridge
Radstock
Somerset & Dorset Joint Railway
Westbury
ARC Whatley Quarry
to Newbury →
to Cheddar
Frome
to Highbridge ←
to Salisbury →
Foster Yeoman Merehead Quarry
East Somerset Railway
Evercreech Junction
Castle Cary
Bruton
to Taunton
to Langport
Templecombe
Yeovil Pen Mill
to Bournemouth →
Sherborne
Yeovil Junction
Thornford
Yetminster
to Exeter ←
Chetnole
Evershot
Maiden Newton
Grimstone & Frampton
Bridport
West Bay
Dorchester West
Dorchester South
Abbotsbury
Upwey
to Bournemouth →
Chesil Bank
Weymouth Town
Weymouth Harbour
ENGLISH CHANNEL
Isle of Portland

0 _____ 10 miles
0 _____ 20 kilometres

Wessex Wanderings
Weymouth to Bristol 87 miles

History of the line

In 1856, after several years' work and delays caused by financial problems, the Wilts, Somerset & Weymouth Railway completed its meandering route from Bath to Weymouth. Apparently built to serve local needs, this rural railway in fact had a significant backer in the form of the Great Western. This ambitious company, keen to extend its influence into southwest England, saw the Bath to Weymouth line, with its links with major east–west routes, as a convenient way into the territory of its great rival, the London & South Western Railway. Through its interest in, and ultimately ownership of, this line, the Great Western was able to run passenger and freight services to South Coast towns and ports, and thus benefit from the growth of tourism in the late nineteenth century. Branches, to Abbotsbury and Bridport,

constructed by small independent companies, also came under GWR control, while in the Frome and Westbury region links were opened with other GWR routes, notably those serving the Somerset coalfield. From Dorchester South to Weymouth, the line was shared by the two companies, and remained so after the formation of the 'big four' in 1923. Even after nationalisation, Western Region trains ran to Weymouth, carrying holidaymakers and passengers for the cross-Channel and Channel Islands ferries. Today the Bath to Weymouth line is operated by Regional Railways, and the few trains that run are well supported by short-distance and local passengers. Freight services and the holiday traffic have disappeared, and so the line exists in that limbo reserved for unprofitable rural railways.

Above *Its days numbered, the once busy signal box at Yeovil Pen Mill still operates semaphore signals in the station area*

Weymouth today boasts a brand new station, a compact structure in brick, built to mark the completion a few years ago of the electrification of the line from Bournemouth. At that point a new generation of high-speed electric trains was introduced, offering a rapid and comfortable service to and from London and making sense of a previously complex operation that involved the use of diesel locomotives to haul the train over the non-electrified section west of Bournemouth. These smart, modern trains, are now primary users of Weymouth station. They overshadow completely the station's only other regular service, the diesel railcars that slide in and out of a bay platform on their way to and from Bristol. This line, which meanders northwards through Dorset, Somerset and Wiltshire, is a tangible reminder of the great rivalry that existed between the major railway companies in the nineteenth century. Weymouth's modern electric trains run over the route developed by the London & South Western Railway and its forerunners, whose London terminus at Waterloo was later the headquarters of the Southern Railway. However, the Great Western Railway also had an interest in Weymouth, and its trains from Paddington ran to the town via Newbury, Westbury, Frome, Castle Cary, Yeovil and Dorchester, a service that also lived on into the era of British Railways. The meeting point of these two rival routes was Dorchester, and the line south from here to Weymouth was actually shared by trains from both companies.

On a map, the Great Western's route to Weymouth can be seen clearly as a predatory invasion into London & South Western territory, and it was certainly this that explained the Great Western's support for a local company, the Wilts, Somerset & Weymouth Railway, whose line from Bath to Weymouth was completed in 1857. The route built laboriously and painfully slowly by this company is essentially that followed by the trains that run from Weymouth to Bath and Bristol today.

This is now virtually Dorset's only railway. The main Weymouth line runs parallel to the coast on its way to Bournemouth, ignoring the county's hinterland. In fact, Dorset was always poorly

Above *Edwardian Weymouth in 1908: a Channel Island boat train transfers its passengers for the next stage of their journey*

Cross-Channel ferries

The major railway companies in the nineteenth century were genuinely international in their outlook and their directors shared the then common dream of uniting Europe, if not the world, by train. At the end of the Victorian period the Channel tunnel seemed a distinct possibility, the key to a whole series of pan-European services that, a century later, are finally being realised.

It was this same desire to bridge national frontiers that caused many of the leading railway companies to become major operators of shipping lines. In the nineteenth century the Great Western, the London Chatham & Dover, the North Eastern, the London & South Western and the London & North Western companies all operated fleets of steamers, on both local and international routes. The south coast of Britain, in particular, had a great variety of railway-owned and operated ports, notably Dover, Felixstowe and Southampton, but the most memorable was probably Weymouth, with its services to the Channel Islands and western France.

Here, in true Victorian style, the trains ran directly to the quayside via a tramway through the centre of the town, a delightful anachronism which remained in service until the final withdrawal of boat trains in the late 1980s. By then the service and the trains were but shadows of what they had been in their heyday, when Weymouth's Quay station was busy night and day with passenger and freight trains operated by both the Great Western and the Southern railways.

served by railways and is unique among counties in southern England in having been left largely alone by Victorian companies. It had its share of branch lines, most of which joined the old Wilts, Somerset & Weymouth route. Two of these, to Bridport and to Abbotsbury, were built by small local companies later absorbed into the Great Western, while the third, and most dramatic, ran south from Weymouth to cross the causeway to Portland. The stone quarries were the main inspiration for this heavily engineered route. All these have gone, although the Bridport branch lingered on until the early 1970s before finally succumbing to one of the last swings of the Beeching axe. Also gone is the London & South Western's branch from Wareham across the Isle of Purbeck to Swanage, although part of the route has since been reopened by the preserved Swanage Railway,

However, the county's primary line was always the famous S & D, actually the Somerset & Dorset, but always known familiarly as the Slow & Dirty. Built partly to serve the Somerset coalfield, this railway operated a network of freight and passenger lines over north Somerset. The Dorset part of its title came from one line that plunged southwards from the famous Evercreech Junction near Shepton Mallet to carve its way across the county to Broadstone, where it joined the main London & South Western route to Poole and Bournemouth. After the formation of the Big Four national companies in 1923, the S & D was operated jointly by the Southern Railway and the London, Midland & Scottish Railway, giving the latter a direct route to South Coast resorts for trains from the industrial cities of the North. As late as the early 1960s, there were many through trains using this. Notable was the Pines Express, a service from Liverpool and Manchester to Bournemouth. Others also ran to southern destinations from Sheffield, Leeds, Grimsby, Lincoln and Leicester, often taking all day to complete the journey. For example, in 1961 the Pines Express left Manchester every weekday at 10.30am, and arrived in Bournemouth at 5.32pm, having come via Crewe, Birmingham, Gloucester and Bath. At Templecombe the S & D met the main line from Waterloo to Devon and

Cornwall, and this small village therefore had a huge station, visited by trains from all parts of northern and western England. Now, Templecombe is just a tiny rural station, for all of the S & D was swept away during the Beeching era and the track which echoed to the pounding of North Country expresses has disappeared back into the fields.

Today the trains from Weymouth to Bristol are run by Regional Railways, a section of British Rail formed to look after all those uneconomic but socially vital routes not wanted by InterCity, Network SouthEast or various other predominantly urban operating authorities. In preparing British Rail for its sacrifice on the altar of privatisation, the government has done its best to isolate and make apparently tempting the potentially profitable slices of cake, stripping them of all those awkward loss-making routes of little appeal to investors. Regional Railways has been left, as a result, with a hotch-potch of bits and pieces that no one else is likely to want, scattered all over England and Wales, and including important cross-country routes, such as Norwich to Liverpool, Portsmouth to Cardiff, and Carlisle to Newcastle. No one in

Above *'Hall' Class 4-6-0 No.6952* Kimberley Hall *leaves Bincombe Tunnel, hauling the 8.20am Paddington to Weymouth Quay on 14 July 1951*

Opposite *One of the last regular locomotive-hauled trains in the region: Class 37 diesel 37421 departs noisily from Maiden Newton station with a Bristol to Weymouth train in the summer of 1993*

Above *Ex-GWR 2-6-0 No.5323 with a freight train at Dorchester West on 10 July 1956*

distinct sections, and the journey is full of interest. The first section, from Weymouth to Yeovil, is carved through the steep Dorset hills, with views out over a traditional and quintessentially English landscape, the skyline broken by old trees and church towers. From Yeovil to Castle Cary the line crosses a high plateau of Somerset farmland and then it moves into Wiltshire and a more conventionally attractive landscape of rolling farmland. From Trowbridge to Bath it follows the dramatic and steadily deepening course of the river Avon, an exciting journey of twists and turns along the steeply wooded valley. From Bath to Bristol, it joins Brunel's justly famous Great Western main line, a route of splendid engineering and theatrical grandeur opened in 1841. On a clear and sunny day in spring or autumn the journey is a delight, a leisurely crossing of the changing landscape of southern England. At the same time, the line serves many more basic functions, the trains taking people to work, to school and on shopping expeditions to Bath and Bristol. In the summer, it still offers the most direct route to the sea for people living in the heartlands of Somerset and Wiltshire. Overall, however, like most cross-country routes, it serves primarily local needs, with far more passengers making short journeys than travelling the whole distance.

On a grey and wet afternoon, with a chill breeze coming off the sea, the 15.00 from Weymouth was surprisingly well filled with passengers of all ages. There was even a drinks and snacks trolley, propelled by a buxom girl who began to ply her trade as soon as the train slipped out of the station. From Weymouth the line runs straight inland, climbing steeply the famous bank up which in the days of steam heavy boat trains had to be helped by pilot engines. Even the diesels of the newish Sprinter-type train labour heavily, grinding their way into the hills. The climb continues past Upwey, formerly the site of the junction with the Abbotsbury branch, and then the train tunnels under the hills. South of Dorchester the Legoland of the new town spreads inexorably towards the great hill that carries Maiden Castle, one of the largest earthworks in Britain. Just after passing a huge

government circles seems to care what will happen to Regional Railways after privatisation. Many of these lines, cut off from central funding and an immediate burden upon local government, are likely to be left to die, with no place in policies that put short-term profitability above long-term social necessity. The former Wilts, Somerset & Weymouth line is just such a route, now facing a very uncertain future. In organisation terms, it is a curiosity, cutting across and connecting with four main lines that run westwards from London, two now in the care of South Western Trains and two part of InterCity's Paddington empire. Its relative isolation and its rural route still betray its Great Western origins. At one time it was a major north–south link for both passenger and freight services, thanks to its important connections, but now all it carries are the eight or so trains that shuttle to and fro between Weymouth and Bristol every day.

It is a railway of great variety, with several

Left *A Regional Railways Sprinter crosses the river Frome north of Dorchester with a Bristol to Weymouth train*

Below *Staff and passengers pose for the camera at Maiden Newton station, once the junction for Bridport, circa 1910*

cemetery filled with extravagant nineteenth century stone angels, the train swings away to the left, on to the old Great Western route. Dorchester still has two stations, the main one, Dorchester South, newly rebuilt in decorative brick, on the London line, and Dorchester West, an original Brunel-designed structure with a typical hipped roof, serving the Bristol route. Looking smart and well-cared for, after years of decay, this building now has nothing to do with the railway, but has started a new life as a Chinese restaurant. Leaving the station, the train enters the tunnel through Poundbury Hill, dug at Brunel's insistence to save the hill fort above from damage.

Following the Frome Valley, initially on a long raised embankment, the line continues through the hilly landscape with views of remote villages and farms. Maiden Newton, a large station with good original buildings and an old signal box, was the junction for the Bridport branch, sections of which

are now an official walkway. It was the Bridport branch that boasted a station called Toller Porcorum, one of a number of splendid Dorset names in this area, such as Ryme Intrinseca, Melbury Bubb and Beer Hackett, names straight out of Thomas Hardy. This part of the journey is marked by the Englishness of its views, with fine houses set in valleys surrounded by specimen trees and copses, the rolling hills of classic hunting country. The spire of Cattistock Church rises above the trees, and then the train passes the site of Evershot station. Still in use is Yetminster, a village station set between two tiny halts, Chetnole and Thornford, in the middle of nowhere. Their continued existence is hard to believe. Like many of the stops along the line, these are by request only. At each one a couple of people got off, to disappear into the grey landscape.

The train passes under the main Waterloo to Exeter line, with a distant view of Yeovil Junction station, and then continues on to Yeovil Pen Mill,

Above *A Victorian scene at the now-closed Evershot station, north of Maiden Newton*

Left *A Bristol to Weymouth train leaves Yeovil Pen Mill. This once busy station still boasts three platform faces and (soon to be replaced) semaphore signalling*

Opposite *Rural Dorset in high summer: Maiden Newton village with a Sprinter arriving at the station*

where plenty of people got off and plenty more got on. Yeovil once had three stations, but the most convenient, Yeovil Town, disappeared in the 1960s along with the line to Langport. Yeovil's variety of stations resulted from its being served by both Great Western and London & South Western trains in the nineteenth century. In the same area, Chard was in a similar position, but none of its three stations are in use today.

The train now gallops across the upper flatlands of Somerset, with no stations to impede its progress towards Castle Cary. To the east the rounded summit of Cadbury Castle loomed out of the grey afternoon light, adding Arthurian legend to the line's earlier links with prehistoric Britain. The train then skirts the mound that carries Castle Cary, before joining the main Paddington to Exeter line just by the station. Here there was another exchange of passengers, and among those getting on were schoolchildren on their way home. The next stop was Bruton, with views of the town's stone buildings spread over the valley. Shortly before the station are the remains of the bridge that carried the old Somerset & Dorset line on its way southwards towards Bournemouth.

A few miles after Bruton, at Witham, a freight line branches away to the west, serving Foster Yeoman's vast quarry at Merehead. The stone from the quarry is carried away on huge modern freight trains, hauled by blue and silver Class 59 locomotives built by General Motors in Ontario, Canada. This line is the remains of the old GWR route to Shepton Mallet, Wells, Cheddar and Yatton, surviving now as far as Cranmore, where a further short section has been preserved by the artist David Shepherd as the East Somerset Railway.

The main line bypasses Frome, but the Bristol train takes the old route through the town, pausing briefly at the station, whose old-fashioned atmosphere is reflected by Brunel's covered train shed roof of 1850, the oldest through train shed still in use in England and a rare survival on a station of

Left *'Hall' Class 4-6-0 No.5996* Mytton Hall *departs from Yeovil Pen Mill with a Weymouth train on 10 July 1956*

this size. Beyond Frome, a line once ran to Radstock, another part of the large network built originally to serve the Somerset coalfield and the stone quarries. The coal mines disappeared years ago, but the quarries are still very busy. Not far from the junction is ARC's Whatley quarry, whose stone trains are hauled by yellow Class 59 locomotives. Westbury is the centre of the stone trade, with miles of sidings filled with Yeoman and ARC stone wagons, and big platforms to handle the routes that cross here.

Passing through Westbury are trains running between Portsmouth and South Wales, and London and the West Country, along with local services. As befits a busy interchange station, Westbury witnessed a complete changeover of passengers. The last of those who had travelled from Weymouth got off, and a new lot crowded on. Leaving Westbury, the train turns off from the main line, taking the branch northwards through Wiltshire farmland to Trowbridge, and then at Bradford Junction it swings westwards into the

Above *An InterCity 125 pauses under the overall wooden roof of Frome station with a summer Saturdays-only train to Paddington in 1993*

Left *A Bristol-bound Sprinter pauses to pick up passengers at the attractive stone station of Bradford on Avon*

Avon Valley. At once the landscape changes, the train following the river as it winds its way along between steep banks densely covered with trees. This is a most dramatic stretch of line, with railway, river and later the Kennet & Avon Canal running side by side to Bath through a region marked by honeyed stone buildings. Particularly attractive is Bradford on Avon, a traditional town that looks good from the train, spreading away from the Brunel-style stone station. Avoncliff is a request stop, and then at Freshford the canal comes into view, the quality of its engineering well shown by Rennie's elegant stone aqueduct that carries it high across the valley, striding over railway and river. Now the line runs between the river and the canal to Limpley Stoke, where there used to be a station and another branch line serving the coal mines. The valley opens out and the train follows the broadening river into a wider landscape. Near

Above *Waiting for the train at Avoncliff Halt*

Right *A Class 37 diesel passes the closed Limpley Stoke station with a Bristol to Weymouth train*

Left *A Regional Railways train alongside the picturesque Claverton Weir between Bath and Freshford*

I K Brunel

If there is one man who stands out from that dynasty of great Victorian engineers, it is Isambard Kingdom Brunel (1805–59). In 1833, he was appointed engineer for the new Great Western Railway Company and under his ambitious and inventive control this line was marked by the excellence of both its engineering and its architecture. Originally built to the unique 7ft 0¼ in gauge, it is still one of Britain's best main lines for smooth, high-speed running.

A man of staggering talent, Brunel was able to design bridges, stations, tunnels, viaducts and complex pieces of railway equipment with equal facility, often using the most advanced technology. At the same time he turned his attention to shipping, his three great steam vessels, the *Great Western*, the *Great Britain* and the *Great Eastern*, laying the foundations of modern trans-Atlantic travel. He had his failures, such as his espousal of atmospheric traction, but his enduring memorial is the Royal Albert bridge over the Tamar at Saltash, a most exciting and impressive gateway to Cornwall.

Bathampton, the old line of the Wilts, Somerset & Weymouth Railway came to an end as it joined Brunel's original Great Western route for the run into Bath.

The approach to Bath is memorable. From a distance the city can be seen spread across the Avon Valley. The train passes through Sydney Gardens in a cutting finely lined with well-cut stone and marked by decorative bridges, and then it rattles through two short tunnels and an embankment, taken over the river by its 37-arch viaduct. From here all of Bath's particular architectural elements can be picked out, one by one, a rich panorama of splendid stone buildings whose familiarity does not in any way diminish their impact. The station stands high above the city, on a curve, with a broad approach avenue leading to its centre. Its grand façade, in a kind of Brunellian Jacobean, shows well how the railway, when it arrived in 1840, was determined to make its mark on the Georgian city.

At Bath the train seemed to empty and refill once again, and then it left with a second flurry of excellent railway architecture, in the form of another great viaduct and the battlemented Twerton tunnel. This paves the way for one of England's best-known, and best-regarded, stretches of railway, Brunel's line to Bristol. Opened in 1841, this maintains his justified reputation as the greatest of the Victorian engineer-architects.

Behind the extravagant stone pinnacles of Bristol Temple Meads station the train stopped finally at one of the sharply curved platforms, still decorated with the Great Western's cream and brown tiling of the 1930s. It was a suitable setting for the end of a journey that has to try to balance the appeal of an unusual chapter of railway history and a rich vision of the English landscape with modern commercial pressures.

The Heart of Wales Line

Shrewsbury to Swansea

SHREWSBURY has a large and wondrous station, a box of delights to tempt the least enthusiastic of railway users. Even at 6.30 on a grey and gloomy morning, the allure is hard to resist. It is the sort of station that makes the perfect starting point for real journeys into the unknown. Its position is excellent, high on the steep slopes above the Severn and well in the city's heart. The façade is commanding, a theatrical panorama of rich Gothic and Tudor details in finely cut stone. Set by the castle, it makes even Bristol Temple Meads look slightly muddled and second rate with its battlements, clocktower and two-storey oriel window. Shrewsbury is a splendid piece of architecture, well proportioned and carefully placed back from the road, a rich backdrop framing a generous courtyard that holds various interesting oddities, including a stone pillar box. It was always impressive, and shows how well the Victorians could handle their architecture. The first version, which was opened in 1848, was an ambitious statement that put on the map little-known and essentially local railway companies, the Shrewsbury & Birmingham, the Shrewsbury & Chester, the Shrewsbury & Hereford and the Shropshire Union. The station later became the hub of a network of railways radiating in every direction, but under the control of those two West of Britain rivals, the Great Western and the London & North Western. In 1904 it was enlarged in a manner that, to the lasting credit of all those involved, not only was sympathetic, but resulted in one of Britain's best stations in the Gothic style. Beyond the façade is the booking hall, recently rebuilt so as to combine

The massive and curving viaduct at Cynghordy, north of Llandovery, on a frosty autumn morning

Heart of Wales Line
Shrewsbury to Swansea 121½ miles

History of the line

Railways came early to South Wales, with many horse-drawn lines being built from the 1820s to service the expanding local mines and to give them an outlet to the ports from which most of the coal was shipped. One such newly developed coal port was Llanelli, which by the 1830s had become the hub of a number of mineral railways mostly controlled by the Llanelly Railway & Dock Company. One of these, opened in 1839, ran to Pontarddulais, from where it was in stages extended northwards to Llandeilo, which it reached in 1857, and Llandovery. In the process it became a fully fledged steam railway, with passenger as well as freight services. For reasons of geography, it fell into the Great Western's area of influence, even though nominally it was operated by the Llanelly Company.

Wales was territory hotly contested by the GWR and its great rival in the area, the London & North Western Railway, and it was the L&NWR, keen to have access to South Wales, that sponsored the next section of the Heart of Wales route. In 1861, the Knighton Railway, a small company apparently independent but with L&NWR support, completed its line from Craven Arms, south of Shrewsbury, to Knighton. Next came the Central Wales Railway, another company in which the L&NWR had an interest, whose line from Knighton to Llandrindod Wells was opened in

1865. Three years later this was finally extended by the Central Wales Extension Railway to Llandovery, where it met the existing line, thus completing a route which allowed the L&NWR access to the lucrative South Wales coal traffic from Shrewsbury. By the time the line reached Llandovery, it had in any case been wholly absorbed into the L&NWR empire.

The 1860s were marked by disputes between the L&NWR and the GWR-backed Llanelly Company. In the 1870s, however, agreement was reached, and from this date onwards the line was in effect operated jointly by the two big companies, a pattern that remained in force after the 1923 grouping, when the L&NWR became part of the London, Midland & Scottish Railway. Even after nationalisation, the Heart of Wales line remained busy with both freight and passenger traffic, and was used as a trunk route. However, the decline that started in the late 1950s accelerated during the 1960s, leaving the line in the uncertain state in which it finds itself today.

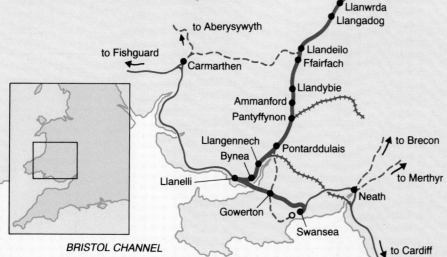

Below *The old signal box at Llandrindrod Wells is now open to the public as a museum piece*

modern efficiency and a degree of traditional atmosphere, with the focus being on the Victorian encaustic tile floor. On the wall there is a plaque giving a brief history of the station. Ideally placed for easy reading while queuing for tickets, it sets the scene for a station that is determinedly didactic.

On the platform is a series of triangular cast iron structures bearing panels listing extraordinary historical facts. For example, in 1848 two navvies engaged in building the nearby Preston Boats iron bridge over the Severn fell into the river and drowned, while in 1866 Shrewsbury gained a second station, known as Abbey Foregate, the terminus for a minor company, grandly named the Potteries, Shrewsbury & North Wales Railway. Familiarly known as the Potts, it had a distinctly chequered career, for by 1880 it had closed, only to reopen in 1911, and then close again for passengers in 1933. It boasted the world's smallest standard gauge locomotive, and an 1844 coach from the royal train, which was still in use when the army took over part of its route in the Second World War. Another panel offered the reader with time to spare some statistics on Shrewsbury's greatest days. In 1932 a staff of 300 looked after the needs of a million passengers a year, and handled 240 trains a week, fifteen of which carried parcels and fish. The panel then goes on to describe a relatively recent station restoration programme, ending with a statement unfortunately now just as out of date as the very idea of a fish train: 'After two decades of indecision on railways, the future now looks good.' Not long ago InterCity stopped running trains to Shrewsbury, dumping the whole station and its complex network of local and cross-country services firmly in the lap of Regional Railways. As a result, its future now looks rather bleak.

None the less, there was plenty going on early that morning, with a choice of pre-7am trains to Liverpool, Cardiff and Birmingham. The snack bar and waiting room was in full swing, and reasonably full of people who had no doubt tired of reading the history panels or admiring the station's fine canopies, mullioned windows and stained glass. Sitting in a bay platform tucked away from the main areas of activity was another early departure,

the 06.55 to Swansea, the first of the four daily trains on the Heart of Wales line. Anyone with a good reason to reach Swansea quickly would do well to avoid this single-carriage Sprinter and travel on the direct service to Cardiff via Hereford and Abergavenny, changing there for Swansea. A delightful anachronism that has lingered on despite numerous closure attempts, the Heart of Wales is a decidedly leisurely exploration of some of the more remote countryside of Shropshire and Central Wales. The train takes four hours to cover the 121 ½ miles from Shrewsbury to Swansea. It serves twenty seven stations, several blessed with names intelligible only to Welsh speakers. The largest town on the eighty miles between Shrewsbury and Llanelli has no more than 4,500 inhabitants or so.

How such a railway came to be built at all is an interesting story, but its survival against the odds is

Above *Ex-GWR 'Manor' Class 4-6-0 No.7802 Bradley Manor (now restored to steam), departs from Shrewsbury station on 28 August 1952, hauling the 3.10pm train to Pwllheli*

little short of miraculous. Reasons such as unusual altruism, or an unexpectedly high awareness of social necessity come to mind, but these cannot really explain the continued existence of a line whose annual costs, about £2 million, are four times greater than its total annual income. The real reason is, of course, politics, in the form of the constituencies through which the line passes, many sufficiently marginal to stop a government of any colour daring to close it. Private owners will recognise no such constraints, however, and the Heart of Wales must be a safe bet for one of the first lines to be closed as British Rail's network is thrown to the jackals.

The reasons are not hard to understand. The 06.55 to Swansea left Shrewsbury with two passengers and three British Rail employees on board, apart from the driver. Throughout the journey passengers came and went, but until the train reached Llanelli there were never more than twenty. In terms of landscape and pure pleasure, the journey has few rivals in Britain, but it is simply too long to have real tourist appeal, too slow to

compete with road transport, and too obscure in terms of the places it visits. Regular sightings of buzzards, and even the occasional red kite, cannot realistically keep a railway open. There is no freight traffic at all, and the modern Sprinter trains have no facilities for the many cyclists who used to travel the route.

The train left on time, rattled slowly out over the Severn and passed the towering brick signal box which, with the network of old semaphore signals it controls, makes Shrewsbury a mecca for signalling enthusiasts from all over the world. There was an entire history panel devoted to it on the platform. In Shrewsbury's heyday, trains converged here from all directions, and even now the signalmen are kept pretty busy. Acres of rusting sidings passed by, populated only by the ghosts of the fish and parcels trains. Among them were the shadowy remains of the former GWR line along the Severn to Kidderminster, part of which is now the province of the preserved Severn Valley Railway. Shrewsbury's suburbs followed, old and new estates interspersed with superstores and golf courses, and then it was out into the Shropshire landscape of distant green hills, twisting rivers, timber-framed farms and old brick barns, rolling meadowlands populated by sleepy horses. Already the journey was taking a step back in time, along an old railway across classic countryside, its links with the past underlined by Great Western wooden wayside signs with obscure messages such as 'Catch Points'. The decorative retro-styling of the new station buildings at Church Stretton and Craven Arms recall the line's earlier days, while at the same time the original stone engine sheds at Craven Arms hark back to the days of steam and all the life that has gone from railways such as this. In those days it seemed that railways were here for good. And there seems to have been so much more time. Old timetables tell of extraordinary, long-winded journeys, such as London to Swansea via Stafford and Shrewsbury, one of the many services routed regularly along the Heart of Wales line. Even more famous is the York to Swansea mail, whose through coaches continued to be attached to local trains until the 1960s. Indeed, it was the

Above *Locally painted sign at Knucklas Halt depicts an ex-LMS Stanier Class 8F 2-8-0 hauling a freight train*

The train also slowed for the first of many ungated level crossings, crawling over farm tracks barely used from one year to another as the driver obeyed the old restriction signs, big iron cut-out numbers in faded yellow. Each one imposed different speed limits, 10, 15 or 20mph, with no obvious reason for the variation. Knighton was the next station, another splendid Gothic structure. Its fine stone buildings with their steep gables and decorative bargeboards, built in 1861 and meant to last for ever, are richly evocative of Victorian Britain. This was this style the Victorians used to conquer the world and the railways, as a primary role-player in the onward march of Imperialism, made much of Gothic. At Knighton the train stopped, and another passenger got on. The station is in England, although the town centre is in Wales, and for the first time there were bilingual signs, such as 'Ffordd Allan' ('Way Out'). How incomprehensible such outbreaks of nationalism would have seemed to the Victorians, intent on uniting not just the British Isles, but the world.

The building of the Heart of Wales line and its subsequent history was certainly a British activity, even if the initial impetus was definitely local. It all started in the 1830s, when a series of freight lines, usually horse-drawn, was built northwards from Llanelli, to facilitate the carriage of coal to the new docks under development there. One of these ran to Pontarddulais, and over the next twenty years this line was gradually extended to Llandeilo and Llandovery, with steam haulage and passenger services being added to the original freight traffic. At the same time the London & North Western Railway, jealous of the Great Western's dominance of the Welsh coal traffic, was keen to have access to South Wales from the north, and so supported the development of a line into Wales from Shrewsbury. The first section, from Craven Arms to Knighton, was built by the independent Knighton Railway and opened in 1861. Another small company, the Central Wales Railway, took this on to Llandrindod in 1865, and three years later this was in turn extended to Llandovery, thus completing a route which, from the start, was largely operated by the LNWR. Only the section from Llandovery

Swansea–York mail that was to be the last steam-hauled passenger service on the line, on 13 June 1964.

Just after Craven Arms, the train branched away to the right, and immediately entered another world. Climbing up into the hills along a single track lined by woodland and old hedgerows, and through a fieldscape scattered with sheep, many of the brown and white Jacob variety, the train began its proper journey through the heart of Wales. Everything so far had been but an overture. Streams and pockets of woodland, coloured by oaks and bracken, accompanied the line as it climbed steadily up the valley, the river's course marked by sweeping horseshoe bends. The first stations, Broome, Hopton Heath and the decorative stone Gothic Bucknell, came and went, the train slowing but not stopping, for these, like most on the line, are request stops only. Old timetables make this point with a particular firmness of manner: 'Calls to set down on notice to the Guard at previous stopping station, or to take up on hand signal to the Driver.' Guessing the identity of the 'previous stopping station' must have added excitement to the journey.

southwards, expanded by the opening in the 1860s of lines from Llandeilo to Carmarthen, and from Pontarddulais to Swansea, remained firmly in the control of the GWR. After a series of predictably acrimonious disputes, however, a *modus vivendi* was reached and, at its peak, the line carried eighteen passenger trains a day in both directions. Its main appeal was the spa towns, with Llandrindod alone attracting up to 100,000 visitors during the season. There were through coaches to Llandrindod from London, the Midlands and many parts of Wales. Even in the inter-war years the Great Western and the London, Midland & Scottish, who had absorbed the LNWR in 1923, continued a successful joint operation of the line until nationalisation of the railways in 1947. In the 1930s there was even a refreshment car on one train each way every day. Freight traffic was also important. Quite apart from the extensive local freight, the line saw several thousand tons of anthracite being taken northwards each week.

Through the 1950s the line remained busy, but it was already being viewed by British Railways as a possible candidate for closure. The first formal closure application was made in 1962. This was rejected, although the lines linking the Heart of Wales route with Carmarthen and Swansea did disappear not long after. Most freight had gone by the mid-1960s. Further closure applications followed, and since then the line has always faced an uncertain future, despite continuing investment by British Rail and the support offered by local councils and organisations such as the Heart of Wales Line Travellers' Association.

The continued existence, albeit in a rather down-at-heel state, of stations such as Knighton and Bucknell bear witness to the ambitions of even the smallest Victorian railway companies, keen to make their mark with distinctive and durable structures. Much of the life they generated may have drifted away, leaving in its wake ghosts and unexpected incongruities – the former goods yard at Knighton, for example, has been completely taken over by a tractors' graveyard. Their survival, however, offers some hope for a better, more sensible future. And that is exactly why all those

Above *The castellated viaduct at Knucklas echoes the nearby medieval castle*

road-obsessed politicians are desperate to stamp the rural remains of our railways into the ground, crushing out the lingering bits of life before that hope takes root. Railways have always been plagued by politicians, and it is not hard to think that Robert Stephenson had the right idea when he drove his engine over one of them at the opening of the Liverpool & Manchester Railway.

Beyond Knighton station the line crosses the river Teme, the border with Wales, and the landscape steadily rises on its spectacular crescendo towards the Sugar Loaf. From Knucklas station there is a view of the suitably picturesque 1864 viaduct, thirteen great arches set beneath castellated parapets and guarded by towers complete with arrow slits, echoing the medieval castle high above. The train climbed steadily, running alongside the river and often high above it, through cuttings and a tunnel to Llangynllo and then on towards Llanbister Road. Here, two smart ladies with Barbours and push chairs got on, and immediately began a long and loud conversation of apparently entertaining intimacy with the guard. For them, the appeal of a countryside of rounded hills and deep

Left *A single Sprinter departs from the isolated Llangynllo station with a Shrewsbury to Swansea train*

Right *A busy period at Llandindrod Wells station as northbound and southbound trains cross*

Below *A colourful display of flowers at Dolau station demonstrates the support given to the Heart of Wales line by the local community*

valleys marked by rivers, churches, old stone farms and an immemorial pattern of fields was overshadowed by familiarity and the chance of a good gossip. Dolau station, at the end of a rocky cutting, is a mass of shiny paint, well-planted tubs and elegant benches, a clear candidate for the Best Kept Station Competition and the pride and joy of the line's Travellers' Association. No one wanted it today and the train drifted through, running on to Pen-y-Bont, seemingly in the middle of nowhere but with a large former goods yard to hint at a busy agricultural past. The train slowed to a halt and the guard climbed down to operate the gates on a level crossing, stopping the traffic to allow the train to creep across the road and into Llandrindod.

It was market day and nearly everyone got off, clutching their bags. The crew disappeared into the station buildings and the train sat in the passing loop, alongside another bound for Shrewsbury. Time passed. Some walkers appeared and got on, followed by a group of girls, and then another driver emerged, young, chatting to a friend, grinning and clutching the inevitable enamel flask. The Shrewsbury train roared and departed, but

Above *Steam returned to the Heart of Wales line in June 1993. Preserved ex-LMS 4-6-0 Class 5 No.44767 George Stephenson, and ex-BR Standard Class 4 2-6-4 tank No.80079 pause at Llandindrod Wells with a northbound train to take water from fire hydrants*

Opposite *A single Sprinter on a northbound train climbs slowly towards the Sugar Loaf tunnel*

Originally the two lines were connected by spurs, to allow the exchange of freight wagons. Passengers could also exchange from the lower GWR line to the Central Wales station via a hydraulic lift. It was the Cambrian Railways line that really served the town at Builth Wells, and so Builth Road has never been anything much. One of the long-standing traditions of railways in Britain is that any station with 'Road' in its name, or more recently 'Parkway', tends to be some distance from the town it claims to serve. Builth is, of course, one of that series of spa towns in central Wales from which the Victorian railways drew much of their revenue.

Crossing the Wye and then running through two short tunnels, the train came to Cilmeri. Near this remote spot is a monument to Llewelyn ap Gruffudd, the last native-born Prince of Wales, who met his death in 1282 at the hands of an English soldier. The train rattled through Garth and Llangammarch, another formerly popular spa, without stopping and then it paused briefly at Llanwrtyd Wells (which claims to be the smallest town in Britain) to take on board a woman with two small boys. They all conversed loudly in Welsh until the guard, himself a Welshman, came along, when the woman reverted to the official language of Wales, and that used when addressing those in authority, English. She then settled down with a racy English novel while continuing to address her sons in Welsh.

Climbing steadily now, the train approached the great watershed of the Sugar Loaf mountain. In summer the train stops at the tiny halt put here for hikers. This was originally opened in 1899 as a staff halt, being used by railway workers employed to pin down the brakes of the heavy freight trains, and, later, by those working on the tunnel (which has been closed at least four times for extensive repairs). The line then plunges into the long tunnel, emerging high on the valley side and dropping slowly towards the afon Bran. Its winding course offers passengers ample time to enjoy one of the best railway vistas in Britain, a panorama spanning the Sugar Loaf, the Black Mountain, the Brecon Beacons and, in the valley ahead, the eighteen stone arches of the Cynghordy viaduct. There were brief

nothing much else happened. Llandrindod Wells has what appears to be an original station, redbrick with a pretty footbridge and fine glazed canopies with stained-glass details, a suitable introduction to a Victorian spa town that owed much of its life to the railway. However, set on the wall there is a curious slate plaque which commemorates the 'Re-Victorianisation of Llandrindod Station August 1990'. This disturbing concept, expressed by a horrendous word matched by its Welsh equivalent, 'Ail-Fictorianaeddio', apparently referred to the recent erection of the canopy, which is not original at all, but was once part of County Council offices. Perhaps it was the same spirit of re-Victorianisation that caused this modern Sprinter train to have a lavatory bowl bearing the legend 'Improved Victory Flush'.

The train waited a while longer and then set off, dropping gently into the Ithon Valley, with distant views of the Rhayader Hills and forests rising from tumbling streams. It passed through Builth Road without stopping, crossing over the trackbed of the former Cambrian Railways line that until 1962 had carved its way vertically through central Wales.

pauses at Cynghordy station, where the walkers got off, and at Llandovery, short interruptions in a steady descent in the shadow of the Brecon Beacons.

From Llandovery, whose station houses the Welsh Railways Research Group, the line follows the afon Tywi into a widening valley, with little-used stations at Llanwrda and Llangadog. At Llanwrda someone had clearly been hard at work with the gardening tools. Llandeilo, which came next, had plenty of station buildings, all rather battered but indicating its former importance as the junction with the old line to Carmarthen. The town stands high on a hill beyond the station, its big church and white-painted, slate-roofed houses commanding the ridge. Ffairfach, a small station in the broad river valley, has one of those bizarrely worded railway signs, in this case instructing the driver to 'Stop - Press Plunger. Obtain white light before proceeding'. When the expected heavenly experience failed to materialise, the train continued regardless, turning south into a soft wooded valley, a pastoral section bordering the Brecon Beacons National Park. Llandybie station, graced with old GWR-style name boards, seems to be in the care of

Right *A beautifully posed Edwardian photograph of Llandovery station, circa 1910*

Above *Double-headed steam special with a northbound train, crosses Cynghordy viaduct on 6 June 1993 behind preserved locos No.44767* George Stephenson *and No.80079*

Right *An InterCity charter train hauled by Class 47 diesel 47820 crosses Cynghordy Viaduct on the evening of 28 August 1993*

Above *Llandeilo station in the 1920s with the meandering afon Tywi in the background. Until the Beeching cuts this station was the junction for a line to Carmarthen*

Spa towns

The Heart of Wales line is unique in Britain in the number of spas along its route. It was this element that helped to ensure its success as a passenger carrier during the latter part of the nineteenth century and the early years of the twentieth. The mineral springs at Llandrindod Wells were known to the Romans, but it was the Victorians who established the fashion for visiting this remote spa, drawn not only by its waters but its good climate, clean air and beautiful surroundings. In 1863 the town barely existed, having only about 250 inhabitants, but with the arrival of the railway it could attract up to 100,000 visitors during the season and the population grew to about 2,000. Hotel porters regularly met the trains, with their through carriages from London, the Midlands and South Wales, unloading often taking up to fifteen or twenty minutes.

Most visitors came by train and it is important to remember that even via Shrewsbury, Llandrindod Wells was only a little over five hours from Euston.

Llandrindod Wells was just one of a series of spas along or near the Heart of Wales line. There were chalybeate, saline and sulphur springs at Builth Wells and at Llangammarch Wells, known for its quiet hotels, its lake and its barium chloride springs, good for heart trouble. The sulphur springs at Llanwrtyd Wells became well known after the Reverend Theophilus Evans was cured by them of scurvy in 1732.

The fashion for taking the waters has past and these little towns, whose visitors now rarely come by train, have become historical curiosities, characterised by the atmosphere, and buildings, of the Victorian era.

the county primary school, showing local support for a line that is essentially a local service. At Ammanford a coal wagon and a plough, painted shiny black, stand on the platform, traditional symbols of agriculture and industry. From here onwards the line is surrounded by shreds of the two great industries of South Wales, coal and metal working, industries just clinging to life in a region devastated by political and economic change.

This was underlined by Pantyffynnon, a proper station with a full range of buildings, an old signal box still in use, some resident staff and a freight yard serving the old colliery branch that is kept alive by the demands for anthracite. Several people joined the train here, giving the single car a decent complement of passengers for the first time. After leaving the station, the line crosses the Amman River, and then follows the widening Loughor towards its estuary. At Pontarddulais the first graffiti appear amid increasingly industrial surroundings, and then the train turned westwards besides the Loughor, setting out on the indirect route via Llanelli, necessitated by the closure, in 1964, of the original, and more sensible Central Wales line straight to Swansea's Victoria station.

With its magic heartlands a fading memory, the line gallops along the marshy fringes of the estuary, passing Llangennech and Bynea and racing towards the sea across a landscape of ponies and herons. At a complex junction curiously like a motorway intersection, it joins the main coastal line for the last few miles into Llanelli, passing the huge bulk of the steel works, miraculously still in business. Llanelli has a surprisingly large station, which has clearly seen better days. Here the Sprinter halted and, as soon as the doors had opened, it filled with people of all ages going shopping in Swansea. All seats taken, it reversed out of Llanelli the way it had come, passing such local delights as the Hotel Miramar and a mobile fish and chip van with 'Frying Squad' emblazoned on its battered sides, to return past the junction where the Heart of Wales line had ended and rattle on to Swansea's terminus station, an ordinary train now, full of shopping bags and the buzz of conversation.

Below *A Swansea-bound Sprinter crosses the afon Tywi, between Llandeilo and Ffairfach, with an early morning train.*

The Cumbrian Coast
Carlisle to Carnforth

THE LONDON–GLASGOW train sweeps into Carlisle half an hour late. Passengers spill out, and those among them, mostly old ladies with bags, who want the Cumbrian coast service to Whitehaven and Sellafield are rounded up by station staff and hurried along to the waiting three-car Sprinter. Thanks to the guard in the London–Glasgow train, who had radioed ahead, this train has been held, and the old ladies' worries, increasing steadily since Crewe, have subsided. One of the ladies, a regular traveller from Birmingham to Sellafield to visit her son and his family, has a long discussion with the guard about the effects of privatisation, and they agree that everyone would be losers, he remarking that as an employee of one company he could not request the holding of a train by another company, and she saying that as the line was likely to close anyway she would no longer be able to see her son and her grandchildren unless they came to fetch her in the car. It was an inauspicious start.

As soon as everyone is on board, the train sets off. Without the contingent of old ladies it would be very empty, the other passengers mostly being girls on their way home to those few outlying villages that still enjoy the benefit of a train service. They all get off in ones and twos at the first few stations. According to the timetable this is the 13.45 from Carlisle to Manchester Airport. On paper it sounds like an efficient, modern service, but one glance at the map and it is immediately apparent how incongruous it is. Anyone really wanting to get to Manchester Airport would hardly be amused by a tour of the Cumbrian coast lasting several hours. What the train really offers is a quick service from Preston to Manchester Airport after an immensely slow, indirect, and completely delightful meander

A northbound single Sprinter hugs the coastline on the single-track section between Braystones and Nethertown

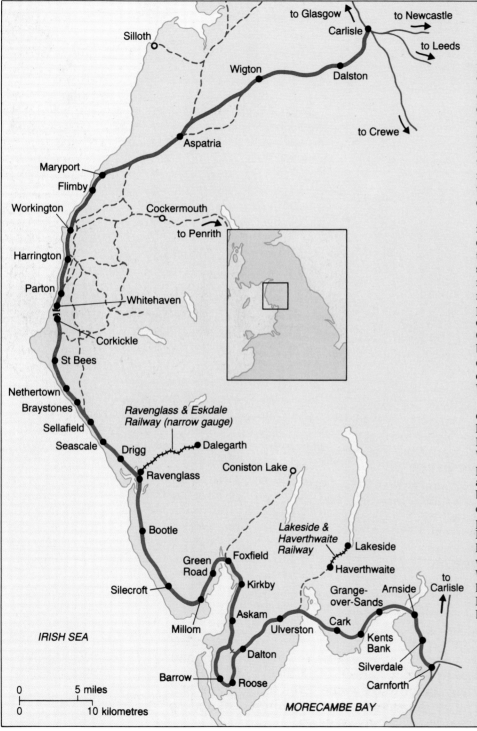

The Cumbrian Coast
Carlisle to Carnforth 114 miles

History of the line

The inspiration for the building of a railway along the Cumbrian coast came from the need to exploit the local mineral deposits of coal, iron ore and, most important, haematite, and then to give the developing mines and quarries an outlet for their products in the Cumbrian coastal ports.

The line that survives today is the scant remains of a once extensive network that covered the Cumbrian hills, built by a series of independent Victorian railway companies. The first railways in the region were planned in the 1830s. One of the earliest was the Maryport & Carlisle, whose coastal route, begun in 1837, was finally opened in 1845 and later extended southwards by the Whitehaven Junction Railway.

The extensive development of local iron ore, and later haematite, deposits, turned Maryport, Workington and Whitehaven into flourishing ports and centres of industry, and the line along the coast became the backbone of a complex network of predominantly mineral lines. Many of these were essentially local lines, but more important was the Cockermouth & Workington Railway, whose lines eastwards to Keswick and Penrith cut through the heart of Lakeland.

To the south was the developing network of the Furness Railway, centred on the rapidly expanding industrial town of Barrow. This ambitious company wanted its share of the profitable trade, and the iron and steel works of its region needed access to raw materials, and so a line was built northwards to Whitehaven, starting in 1845. By 1850 the coastal route was complete, the southern section marked by the many crossings of rivers and estuaries. By buying up its rivals and erstwhile partners, such as the Ulverstone & Lancaster Railway, the Furness developed into a massive railway and industrial empire, and was also instrumental in developing tourism in the lakes and around the shores of Morecombe Bay.

From the 1880s there was a steady decline in the industries of west Cumbria and the local railway networks contracted steadily through the early decades of the twentieth century. With the groupings of 1923, these essentially local railways were absorbed into the LMS, and by the time of nationalisation the pattern of decline was well established. The closures of the 1960s left only the Cumbrian coast line, a struggling survivor of a once great network, kept artificially alive by the needs of the nuclear industry.

from Carlisle to Preston, taking about four times as long as the direct West Coast main line route. The Cumbrian Coast line is unique, an extraordinary survival from another age of railway travel, and offering more miles of seaside than any other railway in England. For much of the journey the train is virtually on the beach, running beside the sea against a backdrop of Lakeland hills. The line closely follows the changing landscape of the coast, swinging inland from time to time to skirt the various river estuaries whose tidal marshlands add a particular quality to a journey characterised by the colour and light of sea and hills.

It is a leisurely train, with a friendly crew taking time to chat to passengers both familiar and unfamiliar. Strangers feel quickly at home, without any of that sense of exclusion found on many local lines, and conversation is easy. The older passengers had come well equipped for a long and lazy journey, and soon the tables hold their share of thermos flasks, home-made sandwiches, and apples carefully prepared by elderly penknives. Some people have maps, but there is a notable shortage of walkers on a route ideal for forays into the Lakes. As ever, the ubiquitous Sprinter trains, with their lack of storage space, have effectively killed off the former traffic in cyclists, leaving the Cumbrian Coast line to the old ladies, mostly on family business.

The lady from Birmingham, her Black Country tones a delightful counterpoint to the lilting Geordie of the guard, falls into a discussion about Sellafield. Everyone on the train seems to know that it is only the nuclear reprocessing plant here that keeps the line open, and there is a general awareness of, but reluctance to enter into, the particularly thorny moral dilemma this poses. The anti-nuclear stance automatically adopted by most people today suddenly becomes less clear-cut when confused by major local issues such as employment and the survival of regional transport; a moral certainty becomes a moral minefield. The Birmingham lady admits that she had been worried when her son and his family moved up to Sellafield, but she is now convinced that pollution levels are higher in the West Midlands.

Carlisle, as befits a border town of such long-standing importance, has a grand station, large, high-roofed, spacious, and solidly built from pale grey stone in a generally Tudor Revival style. From its opening in 1847, it was used by several companies, notably the Lancaster & Carlisle and Caledonian Railways, and its early years were plagued by the kinds of territorial disputes often associated with small and competitive railway companies. Peace reigned from 1861, with the formation by Act of Parliament of the Carlisle Citadel Station Joint Committee. Prior to the 1923 groupings, it must have been a busy place, its platforms being visited by trains from no less than seven companies, the Caledonian, the London & North Western, the Midland, the North Eastern, the North British, the Glasgow & South Western and the Maryport & Carlisle, with their varied liveries adding colour to the scene. Even today, trains still arrive at the station from five directions, and so there is always plenty going on.

Above *Gazing out to sea from a Sprinter near Sellafield*

changing point for a little branch line to Mealsgate. The line continues across the increasingly hilly landscape, the green hills broken by patches of woodland and the browner, harder shapes of the overgrown spoil tips from long-abandoned mines and quarries. Grey stone bridges over little rivers contrast with the red sandstone used by the railway builders. The surviving stations, goods sheds and particularly the bridges across the line, reflect in their simple styles and decorative rustication the high standards and durable qualities characteristic of proudly independent local railways.

The company responsible for this part of the line was the Carlisle & Maryport, and its inspiration was the local coalfield and the rapidly expanding harbour at Maryport which, by the 1830s, was handling up to 100,000 tons of coal per year. The railway received its Parliamentary authorisation in 1837, the route having been surveyed by George Stephenson, and construction began at both ends. Despite initial optimism, progress was slow, and it was not until 1845 that trains were running over the entire route between Carlisle and Maryport. The company's early history was plagued by muddle and incompetence, but in commercial terms it was a success, coal exports via Maryport having more than tripled by the late 1850s.

At the same time, the Maryport & Carlisle began to extend itself southwards, via the Whitehaven Junction Railway, incorporated in 1844 and fully operational by 1847. The opening of this dramatic route, following closely the twists and turns of the coastline, enabled passengers to travel between Carlisle and Whitehaven in little over two hours, but at this date many still preferred to use the well-established coastal steamer services which were, in any case, far cheaper. This southwards extension passed through Workington, and as a result this small town and harbour grew at a dramatic rate to become the centre of an expanding network of predominantly freight-inspired railways which linked it to the coal mines, quarries and iron works inland. Before long, the hills that flank this stretch of coast were to bring dramatic growth to the region, initially through iron and, later, steel. A major area of steel production, established by the

Above *A Sprinter pauses at Aspatria to pick up passengers*

On leaving Carlisle, the train drops down to pass under the main lines, and is then immediately in an open countryside of scattered farms rattling along beside the fast-flowing waters of the river Calden. Stations come quickly, first Dalston, and then Wigton, and at each some of the local girls get off, clutching the fruits of their morning in Carlisle. At both places there are sidings and branches to serve local factories, all now out of use. Wigton Station, all empty platforms and basic shelters, redeemed only by the delicate iron tracery of the old footbridge, is surrounded by factories, some of which could surely make use of the railway.

The train curves south from Carlisle across empty fields and little river valleys, and then swings westwards towards the coast. It does not stop at that wonderfully named station, Aspatria, but it slows sufficiently for everyone to admire another pretty footbridge and the fine stone buildings, simple Tudor Revival of 1841, now largely derelict. Until the 1950s, this was the

1880s, was the manufacture of steel rails for the railways of the world. The huge British Steel plant at Workington is still making rails, another commercial activity that helps to keep the Cumbrian coastal route open.

A look at a railway map of the 1880s shows just how extensive the local network was. The coastal line was effectively duplicated by an inland route that branched southwards from Bullgill, near Aspatria, to run southwards via Marron, Branthwaite, Rowrah, Cleator Moor and Egremont, before rejoining the coast at Sellafield. Other lines linked these vertical routes horizontally; five converged at Distington. Passenger services did operate on all these lines at one time or another, but freight was always their *raison d'être* and the inspiration for the many small companies, such as the Cleator & Workington Junction, that raised the

finance to build them. Within this network were some remarkable gradients, notably the stretch at 1 in 17 at Archer Street, on a line near Harrington, which probably was the steepest passenger train gradient in Britain worked by adhesion.

Most of these lines had only local importance, but at the heart of the network was a route that attracted national attention. This was the line incorporated by the Cockermouth & Workington Railway in 1845, a line whose route eastwards to Cockermouth and ultimately onwards to Penrith via Keswick cut right through the Lake District. It passed within yards of Brigham Vicarage, whose incumbent was the son of the poet, William Wordsworth. Wordsworth campaigned long and hard to keep the railway from the Lakes, but the line was built, and survived until the Beeching era. Ironically, if it were still open today, it would be a

Left *A panoramic view of the railway, station and goods yard - complete with horse and cart - at Harrington, between Whitehaven and Workington, circa 1912*

Above *In recent years steam specials have occasionally been run along the Cumbrian Coast. On 17 August 1991 preserved Class A3 4-6-2 Flying Scotsman skirts the coastline at Parton between Whitehaven and Workington with a southbound train*

vital lifeline for the Lakes, relieving this overcrowded area of the congestion caused by cars and coaches whose impact is far worse than anything Wordsworth could ever have imagined.

Industrial decline and depression greatly affected west Cumberland after the First World War, and the first closures in the railway network of both passenger and mineral services occurred in the early 1920s. This pattern continued and by nationalisation only the most important lines survived. In the Beeching era those were gradually whittled away, finally leaving only the original, Cumbrian coast route still open to traffic and surviving by the skin of its teeth.

The route from Whitehaven southwards has an equally complex history. Already a power to be reckoned with in the 1840s, the Furness Railway had begun to develop an important network of lines in north Lancashire and Cumberland, drawing its wealth from the carriage of iron ore and coal. By

1845 it had reached Barrow and, under the dynamic leadership of its managing director, the tycoon Sir James Ramsden, it had begun the development of that small port into a major industrial centre. It clearly made sense to drive a line south from Whitehaven to make a connection with the Furness, and the result was the Whitehaven & Furness Junction Railway, incorporated in 1845. By 1850 the line was completed, joining the Furness at Broughton, at the head of the Duddon Estuary. The original plan had been for a long viaduct across the mouth of the Duddon, but this was abandoned on grounds of cost. Instead the route was extended by eight miles up the estuary and a shorter, though still substantial, viaduct was built, nearly 600 yards long. Timber viaducts were also built across the other rivers of this stretch of coast, the Calder, the Irt, the Mite and the Esk. Along with the Duddon viaduct, these are the major engineering features of the Cumbrian Coast line.

Thanks to the mineral wealth of the region, the Furness Railway, after a somewhat hesitant start, became one of the most powerful of the smaller companies, retaining its independence, and its Indian red locomotive livery, until the groupings of 1923, when it was finally absorbed by the LMS. Iron ore was the basis for its wealth, but even more important was the discovery in 1850 of vast deposits of haematite near Dalton. Steel-making was then in its infancy, but this discovery and the development of the Bessemer process that used the local haematite, turned Barrow, and its railway, into a boom town. By the mid-1850s, about half a million tons of ore were being shipped from Barrow, and town and railway had become inseparable. The Furness built the town hall, the church, the gasworks and the waterworks, the police station and an expanding grid pattern of housing. Before the town hall was completed, the town corporation held its meetings in the railway offices, and Barrow's growth as a railway town was so rapid, and so dependent upon one company, that it became known as 'the English Chicago'. In the early 1860s, the population more than doubled in under four years, a remarkable growth inspired by the activities of one small railway company in a particularly remote region of England. Thanks to iron and steel, other little villages experienced rapid development into industrial towns. At Millom, near the Hodbarrow haematite mines, the population swelled from 163 in 1863 to over 4,000 by 1876.

The Furness used its wealth to buy its rivals, such as its southern partner, the Ulverstone & Lancaster, and other lines that offered further outlets for mineral traffic. It also constructed vast docks at Barrow, which maintained the town's economic growth to the end of the century. Also important was the arrival of Vickers, introducing ship-building and a host of other related activities, mostly military and naval. The carriage of minerals remained the core of the company's success, but the Furness also became known for a number of other cargoes, including cockles from Morecambe Bay and seaside turf for bowling greens, the latter being loaded at a special siding near Grange-over-Sands. Also increasingly important were passengers,

notably in the form of tourists, and a number of attempts were made from the 1850s to develop the Furness's potential as a carrier for visitors to the Lakes and the seaside. There were plans in the late 1870s to create major new resorts at Seascale and at St Bees, but these were doomed to failure by their relative isolation. More successful were the links to Coniston and Windermere, and the development of more traditional Morecambe Bay resorts such as Cark and Cartmell, Grange-over-Sands and Arnside. Shortly before the First World War the Furness was carrying over 4 million passengers a year, traffic that was, however, strictly seasonal.

The pattern since the 1920s has been one of steady decline for all the railways of west Cumbria. The output of iron, steel and coal has been reduced and all that remains now is the rail-making plant at

Below *Maryport & Carlisle 0-4-2 locomotive No.15 arriving at St Bees heading the Furness Railway mail train to Barrow, circa 1918*

years ago, leaving only a signal box to hint at former grandeur. Gone also is that thrusting spirit of Victorian enterprise that developed both railway and docks, and Maryport is now a quiet place. A couple get off and disappear slowly into the town, and then the train runs towards the sea, drawn by that magic quality of coastal light almost on to the shore. From Maryport southwards the line runs parallel to the sea for miles, with nothing but the waves rolling on to the empty beach. The train does not stop at Flimby, and one has the impression that it rarely does, that no one ever leaves those gaunt grey terraces. The sea is quiet, but on stormy days the waves fling themselves up towards the line, with spray arching over the train. A complexity of old tracks, disappearing into the hills, marks the site of junctions with mineral lines and the route eastwards to Cockermouth, all long gone, and then the train comes slowly into Workington's big and

Left *A southbound Sprinter with a train for Barrow at Workington, once a hive of activity*

Below *The sun's rays penetrate the deserted covered passenger footbridge at Workington station*

Workington. The major mines of the region have closed and other industries have come and gone, leaving as their legacy vast tracts of derelict land. Barrow docks are much reduced, with one rarely used branch linking them to the main line. Passenger services are fragmented, and few trains run the whole route from Carlisle south to Lancaster. Only one thing has kept the line in existence, and that is the nuclear installation at Sellafield, a major industry grown out of the post-war experiments at Calder Hall. With coal driven out of existence by an energy policy heavily weighted in favour of the nuclear industry, it is an irony that British Nuclear Fuels, in an attempt to attract visitors to Sellafield, has from time to time supported the use of coal by running steam-hauled special trains along the line.

At Maryport the train comes down to the sea, pausing briefly at the plastic shed that now serves as a station. The grand buildings that were the pride of the Maryport & Carlisle were swept away

proper station, all creamy brick and bearing a sense of past importance. There are numerous decaying sheds and miles of decaying sidings, scattered with those car breakers' yards and and vehicle dumps that always seem to flourish, like festering sores, on dying railways.

The remaining girls get off the train here, leaving just a few old ladies and a young couple with a baby. Beyond the station is the only echo of the region's industrial history, the British Steel rail plant, still clinging on to life. Flat wagons loaded with rails for railways around the world stand alongside the sea.

The train runs on, right by the sea, following closely the ins and outs of little bays, through one of England's most hidden corners. It stops briefly at Harrington, once a great industrial centre, now a quiet grey place with fishing boats in the harbour and terraces looking eternally out to the empty sea. The Station Hotel carries reminders of the past, with a locomotive in the fiery Furness Railway colours on its signboard. Next is Parton, another secret little harbour and the former site of a junction with lines that led into the industrial hinterland of Distington. Then the train comes slowly into Whitehaven, with views of the old harbours and quays, all tidied up, thanks to a huge EEC development grant.

Whitehaven is a remarkable town, where eighteenth-century formality and elegance are overlaid with Victorian exuberance and twentieth-century indifference. It spreads high on to the hillside behind the harbour, the sort of place to make you leave the train and explore. Old lines lead down to the harbour, the remains of a huge network that grew out of Whitehaven's complex railway history. For originally two lines met at Whitehaven – except that they did not. The one from the north stopped at Bransty, and the one from the south ended well short of the town centre. For a while there were very complicated arrangements for taking trains from one line to the other, with positive links hindered both by local politics and by the band of hills that circle Whitehaven's southern approaches. In the end a tunnel was cut through the hills, and the two lines

came together. Even in its modern indifference, Whitehaven station still feels as though it might once have been a terminus. Just beyond the tunnel is Corkickle Station, set among old branch lines leading down to the sea and inland to the mines. Signal boxes stand as dinosaurs, left-over relics of another age.

From Whitehaven the train turns inland, into the hills and away from the sea as it cuts across St Bees head. This is like an interlude, a conscious change of scene, for when the line comes back to the sea it is a very different railway. Industry and the ghosts of former greatness are left behind, and in their place are the lingering remains of the line's other *raison d'être*, tourism. That is the quality of the journey along the Cumbrian coast, change and variety unrivalled in Britain.

St Bees is immediately different, an old town of rough red stone, with school buildings and big, well-established hotels taking their style from the priory church. The red stone station blends in well,

Above *Signals and signal box stand over the sidings at Corkickle, south of Whitehaven, in silent testimony to busier days*

Right *A Barrow to Carlisle Sprinter approaches the lonely seaside halt at Nethertown*

Below *Braystones station seen in October 1993, gutted by fire*

and there is even a stone signal box. The train waits at the station while there is a leisurely exchange of tokens, the signalman wandering across to hand the new one to the driver, stopping for some banter with the guard, and then climbing back into his little stone fortress. The train slowly moves off and turns back to the sea, to run along the shore, right above the beach. Even the names are different, 'Nethertown' and 'Braystones' echoing those memories of old-fashioned seaside holidays stirred by the faded chalets and huts that sit on the sand, looking out to sea. The guard wanders through, looking for something to do, and falls into conversation with one of the old ladies. He tells her about the quality of light on the sea early in the morning, when the trains are always empty, and there is a sense of sharing a private privilege. The conversation ends as the train comes into Sellafield, and the lady gathers her bags. Her daughter-in-law stands on the platform and the grandchildren begin to jump about and wave. The guard passes out her case, and they quickly walk away, the journey already forgotten.

There are complicated arrangements at Sellafield.

Right *With the chimneys of Sellafield in the distance, a Barrow-bound Sprinter passes the faded beach huts on the coast between Nethertown and Braystones*

The train stops on a single line between two platforms, and the two remaining passengers get out, as it happens one on each side. It then goes off into a siding and collects another couple of carriages. It stands there a while and then returns to the station. There is a long wait, engines idling, the wind blowing in from the sea. A train for Carlisle arrives, pauses and leaves, almost empty.

Suddenly, at first in ones and twos, and then in larger groups, people appear, out of nowhere, and within a few minutes the train is full, every seat taken. Some people are standing. This is the 15.56 from Sellafield, a workers' special. British Nuclear Fuels pays for two trains a day, one up from the south in the mornings, and this one back, and their employees travel free. Any other passengers are simply a little bonus for British Rail.

Hitherto, only the magic of the sea has filled the train, but now it buzzes with conversation and the rustle of newspapers. It sets off, passing Sellafield's distant silver domes and its sidings full of weird-looking wagons, exotic things caged behind high fences, and then it runs on along the shore to Seascale. It was here that the Furness Railway decided to establish a resort, and they built a grand station, a hotel, some terraces of houses and a

Above *Furness Railway 4-4-0 No.37 poses for the camera with a southbound train at Seascale, circa 1914-18*

strange circular stone water tower, which still stands, looking like part of a castle. Despite all that effort, no one came to Seascale, and so it lingers on as a might-have-been, still struggling to attract another generation of holidaymakers. By now the train is silent again, every single person fallen into a deep sleep, collapsed at the end of the shift, and the wonderful backdrop of approaching hills and distant Lakeland views passes unnoticed.

The journey changes again as the line swings into the hills to Drigg, and then across the estuary of the Irt on a long, low viaduct, to Ravenglass. Dunes, saltmarsh, holiday homes and the neat little trains on the Ravenglass & Eskdale Railway set a different

atmosphere. The workers sleep on. At Bootle there is a pretty timber station, like a pavilion, painted green and cream, and another stone signal box. A couple of passengers get on, hitching a ride on the workers' special, and the guard stirs himself to do some work and sell a couple of tickets.

The sea is now out of sight, and the view from the windows is over high hills patterned by sheep and dry stone walls. Silecroft comes and goes and then, as the train approaches Millom, as though by some secret signal, everyone wakes up. They all pour off, to disappear into Millom's grey streets, keeping alive a town created by Victorian industry. Suddenly it is an ordinary train once more, carrying

The Ratty

Known familiarly as the Ratty almost since its opening, the Ravenglass & Eskdale Railway is one of Britain's premier miniature lines, and a journey along its seven-mile climb from Ravenglass up the valleys of the Mite and Esk to Eskdale (Dalegarth) in the Lakeland hills is an essential part of any visit to Cumbria. It all started in 1871, with the discovery near Boot in Eskdale of a large deposit of haematite, the exploitation of which was limited by its inaccessibility. Various railway schemes were proposed, but in the end a quickly constructed and rather primitive narrow gauge line was opened from Ravenglass in 1875, initially for goods traffic. Passenger services followed a year later, but were always erratic. The line had a chequered history, the railway company going into receivership in 1877 and the mining company that provided all its traffic failing in 1882. Somehow it staggered on, relying on the infant tourist trade for its revenue until 1913, when the 3ft gauge line closed for good.

Two years later the remains were bought by Narrow Gauge Railways Limited, a company directed by W J Bassett-Lowke, the model railway king, and the railway was completely rebuilt as a 15in gauge tourist line. Reopened to traffic in 1918, it played its part through the 1920s and 1930s in developing the tourist potential of the region. The early 1920s also saw the opening of a quarry at Beckfoot, near Eskdale, and quarrying activities

Above *R&ER 2-8-2 locomotive,* River Mite, *at Dalegarth station in August 1990*

increasingly dominated the railway. In 1949 it was taken over by the quarry company.

In 1960 the Ratty was bought at auction by the Ravenglass & Eskdale Railway Preservation Company, and since then it has been extensively rebuilt. New locomotives and rolling stock, its attractive route and its pioneering use of radio signalling have made it a firm favourite with both railway enthusiasts and tourists.

a few old people and a group of young mothers with prams, gossiping while the children play.

The train sets off on its eight-mile tour of the Duddon Estuary. There is not much to see at Green Road, but it lives up to its name, and then the line swings across the river Duddon, with views of the hills and the wide waters of the estuary. Here are the remains of the old line to Coniston, served originally by trains from Foxfield, whose old water tower and good range of buildings reflect its former importance. The line turns down the estuary's eastern shore and into the heart of Furness Railway territory. Kirkby-in-Furness and Askam stand looking out over Duddon Sands, and then Barrow takes over as the train runs into a landscape of housing estates, allotments and the dereliction of former industry. Little remains to hint at former glories, when Barrow was the heart of Sir James Ramsden's mighty empire. Then, the station, an Italianate palace in brick, was a terminus in the

Below *Silecroft station staff stand very still for a long exposure, circa 1912*

Right *Foxfield's redundant water tank seen in silhouette alongside the combined signal box and waiting room, built in the distinctive Furness Railway style and still functioning*

hearses have been abandoned, left to die quietly among the trees. The landscape gradually broadens again, with views of the Lakeland hills to the north, and then the train stops at Ulverston.

This is an astonishing station, by far the best on the whole line, and the most imposing building in a small town chosen by the Furness Railway to be the vanguard for its attack on the tourist traffic. Completed in 1873, it is a wonderfully ornate Italianate pile, richly decorated with carved stone details, its platforms still boasting huge glazed canopies supported by delicate cast iron. Quietly decaying, it is haunted by those late Victorian and Edwardian tourists who changed here on their way

Below *A signalman operates the open-air signal levers at a level crossing on the main road between Millom and Silecroft*

centre of the town, its site marked by a clocktower. Today, the train stops at a more distant through station once called, inaccurately and unhelpfully, Barrow Central, now marked by the worst kind of post-war architecture and surrounded by empty and rusting sidings. There are distant views of docks and old industrial sites, and then the train goes on to Roose, through a suburban scene of 1930s houses, supermarkets and a garden centre. A girl on a horse trots past the station.

A mile or so further on suburbia gives way to a dramatic landscape of woods, hills and buildings of dark red stone, the perfect setting for the gloomy ruins of Furness Abbey. The countryside then opens out as the train approaches Dalton, marked by its big church and an excellent Furness Railway red stone station whose Gothic windows maintain the atmosphere of the picturesque. It is now a private house. The line twists on, through cuttings and rocky tunnels, and past old quarries and small fields contained by stone walls. In one, two old

to Windermere and the Lakes, or who came for a healthy stay by the shores of Morecambe Bay. Today, not much happens, and no one gets off to disturb the ghosts. The Windermere branch is no more, but a new generation of tourists now travels along a short part of it in the steam-hauled trains of the Lakeside & Haverthwaite Railway. As the train leaves the station, there are views from its elevated route across the town and the canal to the hills beyond, and in the other direction to the distant sea.

Running free from the hills, the train comes back to the sea, the start of a long exploration of the shores of Morecambe Bay. It crosses the mouth of the Leven on a long, low viaduct and then runs across a landscape of saltmarsh and glittering sea against a backdrop of woods and hills on the other side. Sheep wander across the marshes. Throughout the long journey, the sea has been a constant, but always changing, element. Here it is the sea of traditional holidays, underlined by the seaside houses and terraces that range up the steep hillside setting of Kents Bank. From here onwards the train is almost busy, picking up walkers, teachers going home at the end of their day and deep into the politics of the staff room, and other, obviously regular users who bring to the train a sense of normality. In 1866 Sir James Ramsden opened his Grange Hotel at Grange-over-Sands and developed around it a select seaside resort served exclusively by his Furness Railway. In 1877 the current station was completed, grey stone with careful Italianate detailing, good glazed canopies and, on the seaward platform, Gothic windows to allow passengers a view over Morecambe Bay. The railway company also laid out the elegant public gardens beside the station. Not much has changed, and the atmosphere of the old-fashioned seaside lives on, even if the town's grand hotels now struggle to attract another kind of holidaymaker.

The line now runs alongside the estuary of the Kent, and then it swings across it on another long, low viaduct towards the tall grey terraces of Arnside, across the water. There is a short stop while a surprising number of people get on or off, and then the route is inland again, through woods to Silverdale, whose station now houses a

restaurant. From here the train returns to the sea for the last time, a final look at the saltmarsh stretching into a distant silver grey horizon. The end of the line is at Carnforth, first the huge yards filled with maintenance trains and stone wagons, and then Steamtown, its coaling tower standing proud over sidings where old carriages, wagons and locomotives in various states of decay await their turn in the restoration sheds. In Carnforth's gloomy station, the Cumbrian coastal journey ends at the junction with the West Coast main line. The Sprinter, shaking off the magic and the ghosts of the past few hours, accelerates into normality, once again just a modern train racing on its way to Lancaster and Manchester Airport, that least likely of destinations for one of Britain's most archaic, leisurely and enjoyable railway journeys.

Above *A steam special slogs up the gradient at Plumpton, just after crossing the Leven viaduct, behind preserved Stanier Class 5 4-6-0 No.4767 George Stephenson on 27 December 1980*

Opposite *The grandeur of the old railway companies: a double-headed Furness Railway train at Barrow, circa 1912. The train is headed by two F.R. 4-4-0s with No.33 leading*

West Country Branches

St Erth to St Ives, Truro to Falmouth, Par to Newquay, Liskeard to Looe, Plymouth to Gunnislake, Exeter to Barnstaple

CORNWALL is the only place in Britain where the traditional branch line survives in its original habitat and in its original form. Today, there are three that are still running as they were built, Liskeard to Looe, Truro to Falmouth, and St Erth to St Ives. And there is the line that ran from Bere Alston to Callington, now truncated at Gunnislake. Other West Country railways that were once through routes have been turned by closures into branches, notably the lines to Exmouth, Barnstaple and Newquay. In Devon, the branches to Kingswear and Buckfastleigh live on as preserved steam lines. There were, of course, many more in the region. Gone from Dorset are branches to Swanage, Abbotsbury, Bridport and Lyme Regis, from Devon branches to Moretonhampstead, Seaton, Sidmouth, Brixham, Kingsbridge, Hemyock, Ilfracombe, Princetown and Yealmpton, and from Cornwall those to Bude, Padstow, Fowey and Helston. A journey to the West Country today is a requiem for the lost branch line.

The branches that do survive have a somewhat precarious existence, heavily dependent as they are on seasonal traffic. They still offer that pleasure, now very rare in Britain, of stepping off some mainline express at a remote country station to wait for the branch line connection, with time to sit in the sun and listen to the birds. Traditionally, branch lines have been the last resting place for elderly stock on its way to retirement. In the past it would have been some wheezing tank locomotive and a couple of old carriages. More recently it was those

A trio of 'Bubble Cars' rounds Porthminster Point soon after leaving St Ives for St Erth in July 1993

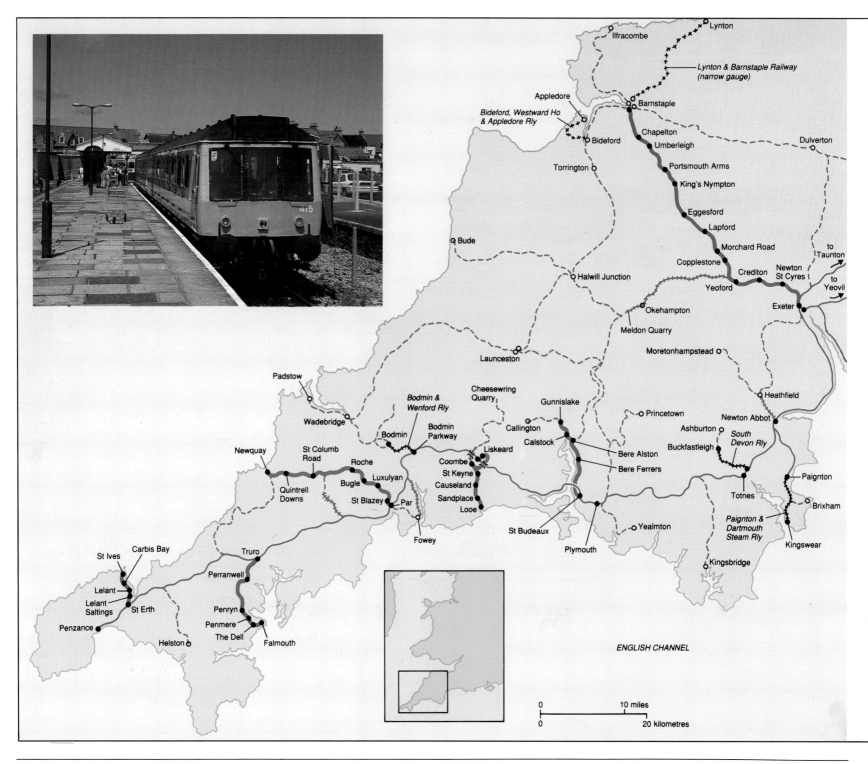

Lynton

Ilfracombe

Lynton & Barnstaple Railway
(narrow gauge)

Appledore

Barnstaple

Bideford, Westward Ho
& Appledore Rly

Chapelton

Umberleigh

Bideford

Portsmouth Arms

Torrington

King's Nympton

Dulverton

Eggesford

Lapford

Morchard Road

Copplestone

to
Taunton

Bude

Crediton

Newton
St Cyres

Halwill Junction

Yeoford

to
Yeovil

Okehampton

Exeter

Meldon Quarry

Launceston

Moretonhampstead

Padstow

Cheesewring
Quarry

Gunnislake

Heathfield

Bodmin &
Wenford Rly

Callington

Princetown

Newton Abbot

Wadebridge

Bodmin
Parkway

Ashburton

South
Devon Rly

Newquay

St Columb
Road

Bodmin

Calstock

Buckfastleigh

Roche

Liskeard

Bere Alston

Paignton

Quintrell
Downs

Bugle

Luxulyan

Coombe

St Keyne

Bere Ferrers

Totnes

Brixham

St Blazey

Par

Causeland

Sandplace

Looe

St Budeaux

Paignton &
Dartmouth
Steam Rly

Fowey

Kingswear

Truro

Yealmton

Carbis Bay

Perranwell

Plymouth

Kingsbridge

St Ives

Lelant

Penryn

Lelant
Saltings

St Erth

Penmere

The Dell

Falmouth

Penzance

Helston

ENGLISH CHANNEL

0   10 miles

0   20 kilometres

West Country Branches

St Erth to St Ives 4¼ miles
Truro to Falmouth 12¼ miles
Par to Newquay 20¾ miles
Liskeard to Looe 8¾ miles
Plymouth to Gunnislake 14¾ miles
Exeter to Barnstaple 38¾ miles

History of the lines

The building of the West Country branch lines spans the whole history of Britain's railways in the nineteenth century, from early mineral tramways to the late Victorian development of tourism and the holiday trade. From the first decades of the century, small, highly localised tramway networks, often horse-operated, were being built to serve the clay industry and the copper and tin mines. From these, lines were then built to serve the rapidly expanding industrial ports and harbours, such as Hayle, Par, Fowey and Devoran. Passenger-carrying did not become important until the late 1850s, when the completion of the main line from Plymouth to Penzance created a backbone to which all the existing localised industrial networks could be attached.

Of the branches that still exist today, the first to be completed were the line to Falmouth, parts of the china clay network north of St Austell, and the railway from Moorswater to Looe, built along the track of the earlier canal. The Falmouth line, originally built to Brunel's broad gauge of 7ft 0¼ in, opened in 1859, was at that time

virtually a main line for Falmouth harbour and the trans-Atlantic steamer services, while the Looe branch was to remain isolated from the main line at Liskeard until the turn of the century. Industry also inspired the building of the branch from Bere Alston to Callington. The next phase of development occurred in the latter part of the century, with the emphasis switching from industry to tourism. By this time, the traditional Cornish copper and tin industries were, in any case, declining rapidly in the face of international competition. The growth of tourism and the conscious development of holiday resorts by railway companies led to the opening of the lines to Newquay and the north Cornish coast, and that classic example of a tourist-inspired line, the branch to St Ives.

Similar developments greatly expanded the railway map in Devon, although many of these lines have since disappeared. The Barnstaple and Exmouth branches, are the remains of an extensive network that developed from the opening in 1851 of the Exeter & Crediton Railway, spreading northwards to Barnstaple and Ilfracombe, and westwards to Bideford, Torrington and the Atlantic coast resorts. The Crediton route became part of the London & South Western Railway's main line to Plymouth via Okehampton and Tavistock, a major assault on Great Western territory. Built in sections through the 1870s and 1880s, the LSWR's main line from Waterloo was finally completed in 1890 with the opening of the section from Lydford to Devonport, built by the Plymouth, Devonport & South Western Junction Railway.

Opposite *End of the line at Newquay. A diesel multiple unit ready to depart with a train to Par, July 1993*

Below *No problems about the Health & Safety Act! A Sunday School outing on the Liskeard & Cardon Railway in Victorian times. This long-closed line was built to link the copper mines at South and West Caradon and the granite quarries at Cheesewring to the terminus of the Liskeard & Looe Canal at Moorswater*

clattering diesel multiple units whose front seats provided a rare view over the driver's shoulder. Nowadays, the Sprinters have largely taken over, but in other respects the joys of a slow and leisurely journey through pretty countryside to a seaside terminus are still there to be savoured. However, if the railway network is further rationalised, branch lines will be an endangered species and these old-fashioned delights will be seriously at risk.

St Erth to St Ives

The journey westwards to Cornwall is one of the best in Britain by any standards, and it is sometimes hard to leave the roaring 125 express at St Erth, knowing that Penzance is so near, and that Mount's Bay beckons. St Erth is in any case a curious station, set among scrapyards and suburban houses, isolated from its village and a seemingly inauspicious place to start a delightful branch line journey. There is a bay platform, set at a lower level and somewhat old-fashioned in its appearance, and it is from here that the St Ives train leaves.

Inevitably seasonal in its popularity, the St Ives branch is nevertheless a line to try at any time of the year. On a clear winter's day the views seem better than ever, and are more easily appreciated in the peace and quiet of an empty train. Just as enjoyable, in a different way, is the hurly burly of the summer, for this is the premier seaside branch line, and sea and sand are rarely out of sight on the 4¼ mile journey.

Today the Sprinters shuttle to and fro, carrying an unexpected mixture of shell suits and Barbours. It has to be said that for people-watchers the train to St Ives has become much more entertaining in the variety of passengers it carries since the opening of the Tate Gallery in 1993, and the line has certainly been busier in the off season. In some ways this has brought back to life the traditional, universal appeal that has been a characteristic of St Ives since the opening of the branch. In the early days, and indeed well into this century, there were services direct to St Ives during the holiday season, with long trains grinding their way round the tight curve linking the branch to the main line. As late as 1961 there was still at least one through train from London, and others offering through carriages. St Ives itself was then a considerable terminus, with ample sidings for stabling long trains and with full facilities for handling steam locomotives. With some trains now running direct to St Ives from Penzance, there is a faint echo of those busier days, but essentially St Ives remains a classic branch line.

On a wet and rather cold summer's day, there were plenty of people waiting at St Erth, not all of whom had come off the London train. As the train came in, the holidaymaking family groups jostled forwards, while the clearly definable Tate visitors hung back, waiting their turn. The driver ambled along the platform to the front, deep in conversation with a colleague, and then, after a long pause, the train set off. Those who had done the journey before took all the seats on the right-hand

Below *4500 Class 2-6-2T No.4564 waits at St Erth station with a train for St Ives on 24 September 1960*

Left *The St Erth to St Ives shuttle, comprised of three first-generation single unit railcars, arriving at Lelant station in July 1993*

Below *A panoramic view of Carbis Bay in 1927 with a GWR train from St Erth arriving at the station*

side, for, in terms of the view from the windows, this is an entirely one-sided route. The clutter of St Erth is quickly left behind as the line curves round towards the Atlantic, and there is a tangible sense of excitement as the great sweep of St Ives Bay comes into view, its miles of sand always alluring, even in the rain.

First the train ran beside the mudflats of the Hayle Estuary, with views across to Hayle, to stop at Lelant Saltings. Here an inordinate number of people stood packed densely along the length of the platform, and they all poured on, battling over pushchairs and shiny plastic raincoats. The explanation for this lies in the very successful Park and Ride system operated from here, a practical answer to the pointlessness of attempting to drive a car through the dense and narrow streets of St Ives. This is a town that would benefit from a total car ban, but there is, as ever, little chance of such a scheme being realised. However, the train is certainly playing its part, and it is cheering to see something so sensible working well.

Opposite *Sun, sea and sand. A St Erth to St Ives train skirts the golf course near Lelant, with Godrevy Point and Hayle Sands in the background*

Left *The Cornish Riviera in the halcyon days of the GWR. A classic view of St Ives station and Porthminster Sands in 1928*

The next station is Lelant, its buildings now a private house. With the church in view high above the line, the train climbs to its magnificent elevated route along the side of St Ives Bay. From here on it is a panorama of delight, a distant view across the bay to Godrevy Point and its lighthouse, and down below great stretches of sand, first Porth Kidney and then Carbis Bay, with the waves rolling in. The railway winds its way among the rocks, closely following the coastline and well above the holiday hotels and old villas that have retained some lingering sense of pre-war style. There is a small station to serve Carbis Bay, and then, with St Ives well in view, the line rounds the final hurdle of Porthminster Point.

It has to be said that St Ives station, once a classy seaside terminus, is now a great disapppointment. It is no more than a series of temporary-looking structures, driven back from the town by a wretched car park that has usurped the station's former site. The train came to a halt at the buffers in the middle of nowhere, and the passengers, a straggling army ringing with the shouts and cries of querulous children, wandered off towards the town. Another army, even more damp and quarrelsome, filled the train for the return journey. At St Ives, an old-fashioned branch line lives on, playing its vital supportive role both for the community and for the thousands of transient visitors who invade the town throughout the year.

Truro to Falmouth

Railways came early to Cornwall, but the first lines were essentially local, built mainly to serve the needs of industry. In the eighteenth and early nineteenth centuries there was extensive exploitation of Cornish copper and tin deposits, and primitive tramway networks were used to move the ore from the mines to the rapidly expanding harbours such as Hayle on the north coast or Devoran on the south. It was not until 1859 that the line between London and Penzance, built in sections by a number of small companies, was finally completed. Notable among these were the Cornwall Railway and the West Cornwall Railway, responsible for the creation, between 1852 and 1859, of the line that crosses the country's spine from Penzance to Saltash.

The one thing all these independent lines had in common was the presence, and driving inspiration, of the engineer Isambard Kingdom Brunel. His remarkable Royal Albert Bridge at Saltash, completed shortly before his death in 1859, is his greatest achievement, and its high crossing of the Tamar was the final link in the chain of railways that connected Cornwall to London and the rest of Britain. However, Saltash was not alone, and it is the viaducts built to carry the railway across the hills and valleys of Cornwall that contribute so much to the journey westwards from the Tamar. Between Saltash and Truro there were thirty-four major viaducts in fifty miles, all designed by Brunel and many built wholly or partially from timber. Brunel developed a remarkably inventive and durable method of building these major structures from yellow pine, enabling the companies with limited funds to complete their heavily engineered routes. None survive today in their original form, having been gradually replaced by brick or stone structures, but the last, College Wood Viaduct, on the Falmouth branch, was not finally rebuilt until 1934. Thanks to these viaducts, and the railway's elevated route across Cornwall, the journey is constantly exciting, offering a sequence of splendid views that is without rival in England. The landscape is continually changing, and with the sea never far away, the quality of light is particularly special. Always exciting is the view of Truro, contained within the curving embankment that carries the train above the city limits. At its heart is J L Pearson's great late nineteenth-century cathedral, the first to have been built in Britain since St Paul's and one of the most magnificent triumphs of Victorian architecture. There are some classic cathedral views from trains, notably Durham, Ely and Worcester, and Truro has to be among this exclusive group.

Truro station is the place to change for the Falmouth branch. Planned by Brunel, and completed in 1859, this 12¼ mile journey, with its eight viaducts, maintains the dramatic approach to engineering and landscape established for the main line. In some ways more main line than branch in its early days, the railway was built to serve Falmouth docks, and in particular the trans-Atlantic steamers that sailed from there. Boat trains to Falmouth were, for a while, a regular feature of the timetable. Even after the boat trains had disappeared, the docks remained busy, turning the Falmouth branch into an important carrier for both

Below *5700 Class 0-6-0PT No.4622 departs from Truro on 8 April 1960 with a Falmouth train, while 4-6-0 Castle Class No.4083, Abbotsbury Castle,* waits to depart on a down empty van train

Left A Sprinter crosses Perranwell viaduct with a Falmouth to Truro train in July 1993. The ivy-clad piers of the Brunel-designed wooden viaduct can be seen alongside

passengers and freight. In the early 1960s some summer trains still had through coaches from London. Today, this is all history and Sprinter units offering a traditional branch line service are the only traffic on the line.

Unlike the other West Country branches, the Falmouth line is not particularly seasonal and it plays an important role in the community throughout the year. It is a line that carries people to and from school or work and takes them out for shopping trips and social events, generally fulfilling the conventional needs of a rural community. Closing such lines only makes more people housebound and forces more cars on to the roads, considerations disregarded by politicians driven by short-term concepts of profitability. The local community of today was well represented by the mix of passengers on the 16.05 – schoolchildren, young mothers with small children, shopping and pushchairs, the usual scattering of elderly people, and some others in that indefinable category known broadly as professional. The guard moved among them, chatting all the while; as he seemed to know nearly everyone, his progress through the train was rather slow. In his late forties, he had served this and other local lines for much of his working life and, like others in his position, was well placed to observe the changing local scene. Travelling up and down over a period of years, he had seen young

children going to school and then to work; he had then watched their progress through the stages of courtship and marriage until they had children of their own. A local train, unchanging, always there, and taken completely for granted, is perfect for a dispassionate observation of the patterns of social life. The guard had a long conversation with an old friend who asked about his wife, somehow making it clear that he had met and courted her on this train, travelling to and fro each day between Truro and Falmouth.

Below Penryn station at the turn of the century. The wide gap between the platforms originally accommodated the 7ft 0¼in broad gauge track

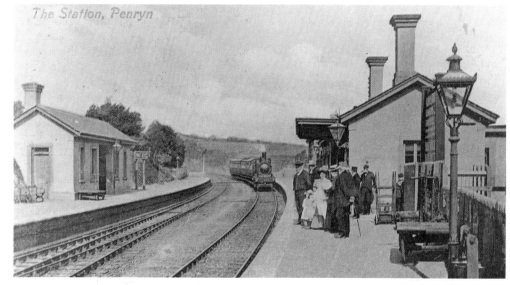

The Station, Penryn

Right *A Truro to Falmouth Sprinter crosses Penryn viaduct. The piers of the old timber viaduct are much in evidence*

Above *Desolation Row - end of the line at Falmouth*

The train follows the main line westwards, then branches away south, with good views from the elevated track over wooded valleys and fields of fruit trees. The route is dramatic, and includes both tunnels and high viaducts. Beside some are the old ivy-clad piers that supported Brunel's original timber viaducts. Just before the little station at Perranwell there is a magnificent view down into the steep Devoran Valley. Until closed by the silting up of Restronguet Creek, this was a major harbour with its own railway network linked to the Falmouth branch and an iron industry that exported steam engines all over the world.

The next station is Penryn, its town spread attractively in the valley below, and then the train makes its rather private entry into Falmouth, via Penmere, the line flanked by back gardens and discreet suburbia. The line ends at Falmouth station, a sad place, its old buildings and disused sidings giving little hint of the town's more attractive qualities, its great harbour and the famous castles that guard it. The line that used to serve the harbour, rusted and derelict, leads away from the station, waiting in vain for a change of policy that might bring it back to life. There has been much talk of a new container port, but the vision of long trains of containers making their way up the Falmouth branch behind a mighty diesel locomotive is still a dream, perhaps never to be realised.

Par to Newquay

The holiday trade was always close to the Great Western Railway's heart, particularly during the heyday of the late nineteenth and early twentieth centuries, and Newquay was one of a number of West Country resorts largely developed by the railways. Expresses bringing holidaymakers from London would leave the Great Western's main line at Par and swing southwest across the Cornish hinterland to meet the Atlantic at Newquay.

In those days, while this was the destination for most long-distance trains, it was not actually the end of the line, for another route from Newquay meandered its way southwards through Perranporth and St Agnes before rejoining the main line at Chacewater. This also enjoyed its share of the holiday traffic, but it was a small share, which dwindled steadily from the 1930s until the line was finally swept away during the Beeching era.

The background to those lines lay in the fierce battle that raged during the latter part of the

Above St Blazey station in 1904, with a train for Newquay waiting to depart. The engine shed, in the background, is still used as a diesel stabling point

nineteenth century between the Great Western and the London & South Western Railway, two great rivals determined to dominate the West Country holiday traffic. The LSWR dominated the Dorset coast and much of Devon, its empire spreading westwards along the coast from Barnstaple and Bideford to Bude and Padstow in Cornwall. The GWR held Somerset and South Devon, and all of Cornwall west of the river Camel. Each had driven lines into the other's territory, vanguards, perhaps, for an expansion that never came. The GWR route to Barnstaple via Taunton was one such incursion, as was the LSWR line to Wadebridge and Padstow. There was some common ground, and the rival routes met at certain strategic points, notably Exeter, Plymouth, Launceston and Bodmin. The

Left 4500 Class 2-6-2T No.5526 on a Par to Newquay train at St Blazey on 5 July 1955. The stream is running with china clay effluent

growing holiday traffic was the primary incentive, but also important were the freight cargoes, notably china clay, which had taken over as the West Country's primary mineral after the collapse of the copper and tin industry. The GWR held most of the clay region, but the LSWR was able to get into this particular act south of Bideford and to the north of Bodmin.

The continuation of this rivalry after the 1923 groupings and into the post-nationalisation British Railways era was reflected by those great holiday expresses, the Cornish Riviera and the Atlantic Coast, setting off respectively from Paddington and Waterloo. Today, the train to Newquay that wanders to and fro along what is now a very minor branch line is a somewhat pale echo of those colourful days of company rivalry, especially during the winter timetable. However, on Saturdays during the summer season the line is visited by InterCity 125s with Holidaymaker trains from Edinburgh, Leeds and Paddington.

Taking a train to Newquay in the middle of the day and outside the high season can be a rather lonely experience, allowing ample time to study the extraordinary nature of the landscape and chat with the guard about the future, and the past, of lines such as this. It is actually quite difficult to sit in any train surrounded by maps, guides and note books without attracting someone's attention, particularly if not dressed in the characteristic uniform, and accompanied by the standard paraphernalia, of the railway buff. Guards, fearing some kind of unofficial, or even official but secret, survey, often make a very direct approach, only cursorily wrapped up in polite curiosity. The slightly aggressive tone of the enquiries made by the guard on the Newquay train suddenly mellowed into one of indifference at the mention of a book, as ever, and the conversation then ranged freely over a number of topics, including memories of St Blazey shed in steam days, and his activities as an accomplished painter of railway scenes. This shed, now used as a stabling point for diesel locomotives used on the china clay trains, is a brick-built semi-circular structure dating from the early days of the Cornwall Railway, one of the best in Britain.

Above *4500 Class 2-6-2T No.4552 on a Par to Newquay train near Luxulyan on 9 July 1955*

It is easy to imagine the curving row of locomotives waiting for the turntable, smoke and steam drifting into the early morning sky. It stands by the track as the train starts the steady climb into the woods alongside a fast-flowing little river. Visible from the train are the remains of old mine tramways, one of which climbs up to cross the valley on the Treffry viaduct, whose great stone arches, built in 1825, stride across the river and the railway. The complex network of such tramways, built initially to carry the ore from copper and tin mines down to the coastal ports, laid the foundation for all the railways of west Cornwall, which remained self-contained and isolated from the rest of England until 1859.

At the first stop, Luxulyan, no one got on or off, and then the train climbed up out of the valley and on to a wilder landscape of rolling moorland bounded by the extraordinary horizon that is formed by the shining spoil tips of the china clay

Opposite *An early morning Par to Newquay diesel multiple unit leaves exhaust fumes in the clear air as it climbs out of the verdant Luxulyan Valley in July 1993*

Left *'Hall' Class 4-6-0 No.5969* Honington Hall *traverses St Dennis Junction with the 4.5pm Par to Newquay train on 11 July 1955. The train includes three through coaches of the Cornish Riviera Express. In the background a china clay train stands on the line from Parkandillack*

Others are still busily in use, notably the line from Burngullow Junction, west of St Austell, up to Parkandillack. If the missing link to St Dennis Junction was reopened then this would make an alternative and more direct route to Newquay. Indeed, there are plans to make this the passenger line, with Newquay trains starting from St Austell instead of Par, and to close part of the existing route so that only that section required by the clay industry, from Bugle south to Par, is left open.

To the north the horizon is marked by distant hills, one of which is crowned by an Iron Age hill fort, Castle-an-Dinas, which for a long time was believed to have links with King Arthur. The next station is St Columb Road, and from here the landscape softens as a sequence of gentle hills takes

Below A Par to Newquay diesel multiple unit nearing the end of its journey as it crosses Newquay viaduct

industry. This is the heart of china clay territory, and it is the needs of this mighty industry that keeps the Newquay line in business. There is a constant traffic of the special clay trains to and fro, linking the pits with the harbours at Fowey and Par, and carrying clay products in bulk to other parts of Britain, notably Staffordshire, where potteries have been dependent upon Cornish clays since the late eighteenth century.

The clay industry adds a particular quality to the moorland landscape, making it unlike anything else in Britain. Distinctively exciting in its colour and light, it adds interest to the remote wilderness that surrounds Bugle and Roche. The demands of the clay industry encouraged the building of a complex network of branches and link lines which riddled the hinterland to the north of Par and St Austell. The remains of those that have gone can often be seen, old overgrown branches and abandoned tracks through the moorland to forgotten freight depots such as Carbis, Carbean and Gunnheath.

over from the moorland. The line winds its way through these hills, and after Quintrel Downs station there are glimpses of the Atlantic ahead as the train rattles on towards the end of its coast to coast journey.

The approach to Newquay is domestic and low key, with no hint of the romance that must have accompanied pre-war journeys to this once great resort. It is hard now to imagine the dark green Great Western locomotives bringing a long rake of brown and cream coaches to a halt and the platforms filling with elegantly dressed holidaymakers. Today, Newquay station is very much the rather tatty end of a little-used branch line, and the few passengers that wandered off into the town were clearly neither elegant nor holidaymakers. Newquay has, of course, developed a new life as a major surfing centre, and this bright but arcane world has overlaid the town's fading charms. However, surfers do not travel by train.

China clay

Cornwall's massive deposits of china clay were first discovered in the middle of the eighteenth century by William Cookworthy, but it was not until the end of that century that they were first exploited commercially, by companies formed largely by Staffordshire potters. The development and rapid spread of English bone china from the 1790s was entirely dependent upon the availability of suitable clays, and so from that date Cornish clays were regularly transported to Staffordshire. They were taken by ship from the new china clay ports at Par, Fowey and Charleston to Liverpool, and thence to Staffordshire via the Trent & Mersey Canal. Cornish clays were a vital ingredient in all kinds of porcelain, stoneware and white earthenware and by the early nineteenth century this was already a huge and complex operation. The first railways were the local tramways, mostly horse-drawn, built to transport the clay from the pits but, with the completion of the main line to Cornwall in 1859, a vast new transport industry rapidly developed. Clays were carried by rail, to the ports for onward shipment to British and overseas ports, and directly to Staffordshire and other pottery-making centres in trains of specially built wagons. From that point on, clays have remained a major bulk cargo and an important source of income for the railways. Even today, with clay being used in many industries besides pottery, including paper making, Cornish clay trains are a significant part of the region's economy.

A feature of the West Country railway network has always been the special clay lines, with their distinctive locomotives and wagons. In their heyday in the late nineteenth century, these were large networks, notably north of St Austell and north of Bodmin, the centres of production of both china clays and other clay types. Today, the Bodmin to Wenford Bridge line has disappeared, but many clay-only freight lines are still in use in south Cornwall. Indeed, it is the clay industry that has helped to keep open the lines to Newquay and Looe, with major pits or drying plants at Goonvean, Parkandillack, Pontsmill, Goonbarrow, Moorswater and the freight-only line to Fowey Harbour.

Below *Class 08 0-6-0 diesel shunter No.08955 shunting china clay wagons at Carne Point, Fowey, on the freight-only line from Lostwithiel*

Liskeard to Looe

Delayed for twenty minutes by what the guard referred to as 'the removal of a drunkard from the train', the Penzance-bound 125 rushed into Liskeard, paused briefly and with a sense of impatience while a few people got off, and then roared off into the setting sun. Nearly everybody walked up from the platform, got into waiting cars, and drove away. Silence descended again, overlaid by insects and birds enjoying the warm late summer evening. An elderly couple stayed on the platform a while, and then wandered slowly up to wait for the Looe train. This, the most classic of all West Country branches, departs from what is, in effect, a separate station. Timber buildings with white-painted weatherboarding, a single platform and some aged seats establish the perfect branch line atmosphere. A few people were waiting, in the soft evening light, for the 18.05, the last train to Looe. Presently it came into view, preceded by the noisy clattering that identified it as an ancient diesel multiple unit, working out its last years on Cornish branch lines. The driver got out, went into the station to replenish his tea thermos, and then walked briskly to the other end of the train. Everyone climbed into the front carriage, the first on board claiming the seats with the view, directly behind the driver. The couple from the London train, who seemed to know what they were doing, went to the rear and settled themselves into the seats that looked out through the driver's compartment at the other end. There was the usual exchange of buzzing between guard and driver, and then the train started with a jolt, setting off immediately down the steep gradient that curves away from the station. It rattled and lurched, its wheels grinding on the steep bends, with the abundant hedges on either side virtually brushing the carriages. The line curves on round and down, and suddenly the viaduct comes into view, its great arches carrying the main line across the valley. The train passed through one of the arches, 200 feet below the station that was already over half a mile away up the track.

The train continued its curving descent, its brakes hissing as the wheels bounced over the joints in the rails, and then, before the small halt at Coombe, it came to a stop in the valley bottom, just beyond a set of points. The guard climbed down, unlocked the frame and operated the point lever while the driver walked back through the train to the compartment at the other end. The elderly couple, smug in their knowledge, sat back to enjoy what was now the front seat. The train started back again, swung right at the points, paused for the guard to climb back on and then rattled off down the valley.

When the Looe branch was built in the middle of the nineteenth century, it simply ran along the valley from Looe to Moorswater and into the hills at Caradon. The complicated link to the main line at Liskeard was added in 1901, chiefly to give direct access to the huge clay works at Moorswater, the main reason for the railway's existence. It is still in use, although the section to the mines of Caradon has long since closed, and the Looe line is therefore unusual among branches in having an active freight life. It is also unusual in that it was built as the Liskeard & Looe Union Canal, opened in 1828, to transport initially sea sand (then used as a fertiliser) and later copper ore from Caradon Hill. The canal was very successful for a while, and then in 1860 its owners opened a railway that ran beside it. Some of the canal was destroyed in the process, but a few

Below *4500 Class 2-6-2T No.4552 arriving at Liskeard with a train from Looe on 15 July 1960*

driver hooted, to encourage them to move in time.

As this was the last down train of the day, it did not stop at any intermediate stations, but the speed was so leisurely that there was ample time to enjoy the views of the widening valley and the surprising number of stations that still survive. St Keyne came next, with Paul Corin's Magnificent Music Machines almost next door, and then Causeland, a flowery station with a direct link to the nearby holiday home development. The appeal of the Looe Valley is obvious, and it is well marketed, with an extensive literature of maps and guides aimed at both walkers and cyclists that makes the most of the train as the starting point for excursions.

Below 4552 again: this time on a Liskeard to Looe train near St Keyne on 18 July 1960

boats continued to use it until 1909, when the GWR took control of the railway. The old canal bed, thickly overgrown, and the remains of a couple of locks can still be seen beside the line, but a more obvious clue lies in the occasional double-arched bridges, the later railway bridge being attached to the original canal arch. There are a number of railways in Britain built on top of former canals; because of its scale and its setting, this is one of the most attractive, and the most enjoyable to explore.

The Looe Valley Line, as it is rather grandly called today, is one of those railways that is good to see at any time of year. In the spring the lineside flowers are mostly blue in colour, but by late summer it is the pinks that dominate the hedgerows, Himalayan balsam and rosebay willow herb.

The train almost made its own way on, gently descending the valley. The driver swatted lazily at a wasp with his newspaper, and the seagulls that stood on the tracks flapped slowly into the air as the train was almost upon them. Once or twice the

The river widens steadily and at Sandplace becomes a tidal estuary, swans mingling with the seabirds and waders on the mudflats. The name 'Sandplace' commemorates the old trade in sea sand, and it was here that barges were loaded and unloaded. All this is long gone and the only industry here today seems to be a thriving trade in garden gnomes. Drifting gently along the water's edge, the train offers a wonderful view over the estuary and its moored boats, and ahead to East and West Looe, divided by the river's mouth. The end of the line comes rather suddenly, the train stopping at the buffers beside a typically basic

station. At one time the railway continued into East Looe and to the quay, to serve the ships in the then busy harbour.

Having come down almost empty, the train was greeted by a dense throng of people, walkers and family groups, who crowded on and quickly filled every seat on the last service of the day back up to Liskeard. Clearly, the promotional literature is having some success, even if, in the process, train travel is becoming a novelty rather than a necessity.

After a few minutes' wait the guard buzzed, and the driver took the train slowly back up the valley, into the golden evening light.

Above *A popular engine on the Looe branch – No.4552 with a pick-up goods arriving at Looe station on 18 July 1960*

Opposite *A Liskeard to Looe train slows for the road crossing beside the East Looe River between Sandplace and Looe in July 1993*

Above *Push-pull fitted Class 02 0-4-4T No.30183 on the 3.15pm Bere Alston to Callington mixed train at Gunnislake on 21 September 1955*

Plymouth to Gunnislake

The 13.45 pulled out of Plymouth's large and rather characterless station on time, with the usual complement of elderly couples, ladies with shopping bags and mothers with young children, that somewhat unrepresentative cross-section of the travelling public which seems to be the mainstay of British Rail's lesser routes. The guard moved among them, stopping for a brief word or two every now and then, as the Plymouth suburbs rolled past, unnoticed. No one bothered to look out of the window at the city's skyline of church spires and towers, and no one seemed to be remotely aware of the rather exceptional nature of the journey that they were starting.

The Plymouth to Gunnislake route has some claims to be one of the most unusual in the British Rail network, a real old-fashioned branch line serving nowhere in particular, and with no obvious justification for its continued existence. It must be, in harsh economic terms, a dead loss and, apart from the series of wonderful views it offers those few who stray upon it, it cannot hope to do much for any potential post-privatisation operator. Landscape and rivers, country houses and history line the route, and included among them, for those who look, are plenty of clues as to why the line was built in the first place.

Plymouth to Gunnislake today bears little resemblance to what was built in the nineteenth century, and its history is quite complex. Part of the line, from Bere Alston southwards, was the final section of the London & South Western Railway's main line to Plymouth, built as a direct challenge to the Great Western's dominance of southwest England. For about a century rival expresses raced each other across Devon from Exeter to Plymouth, two routes that separately avoided the unbridgeable wilderness of Dartmoor. The Great Western took the southerly route, via Newton Abbot and Totnes, which, with its many branches, controlled access to the coastline that the railway company came, in due course, to market as England's Riviera. Stripped of most of its branches, this is today the only line to the West Country. The LSWR, arriving later, had to take the harder route to the north, via Crediton, Okehampton and Tavistock, and then drive long tentacles out to claim a foothold on the Atlantic coastline. This situation remained unchanged until the 1960s with the rival trains, first of the Great Western and the Southern Railways, and then, after nationalisation, of different regions of British Railways, setting off from Exeter and meeting again at Plymouth. Dr Beeching put an end to all this by removing from the map all those routes west of Exeter operated by the Southern Region, with the exception of the line to Barnstaple. From then onwards, the only way to Plymouth was from Paddington.

For reasons that are completely unclear today, a fragment of the Southern's former main line was left in place, running north from Plymouth along the Tamar, not, as might have been useful, to Tavistock, but as far as a small village called Bere Alston. Here, the old main line had met a wandering little branch that crossed into Cornwall and climbed up into the wild hills around Calstock and Callington to provide an outlet for a group of mines and quarries. The next few miles of this were chopped off, isolating it from those mines and quarries that had brought it into existence in the first place. The legacy of Dr Beeching's activities, an unexpected survivor of the massacre, is therefore a long branch line from Plymouth to Gunnislake.

The 13.45 ran on through a cutting that isolated it from Plymouth, pausing briefly at a series of rather unpromising halts, Devonport, Dockyard and Keyham, famous names but seemingly little used today. After Keyham a freight line branched away towards the naval dockyard. There were now good views towards the yards, with warships at anchor and at the quays, but no one on the train paid much attention, having seen it all many times before. Swinging across the main line, the train clattered on to the branch leading away to the north. The change was immediate and dramatic.

Single-tracked, the line quickly leaves Plymouth behind and is soon into more old-fashioned surroundings. There was a brief pause at St Budeaux while the last of the mothers got off with her two small babies, the guard passing down first the babies and then the pushchair. Despite its small size, St Budeaux has managed to retain two stations, Ferry Road on the main line, and Victoria Road on the branch, and it is impossible to travel from one to the other by train. The train drops down to pass under Brunel's Royal Albert Bridge, curving high above on its approach to the Tamar

Below *Bere Ferrers station and signal box. While trains still stop here, the buildings are now in private ownership*

Opposite A Gunnislake to Plymouth Sprinter slowly crosses the river Tamar on the magnificent Calstock viaduct in July 1993

crossing. This unexpected version of a very famous railway view alone justifies a trip on the Gunnislake branch, particularly as you look back towards the bridge and the newer road bridge alongside. This is the first of a series of memorable views. Next comes the broad expanse of the Tamar Estuary, with lines of moored boats against a background of woodland. The line runs alongside the Tamar, in and out of the trees, and suddenly a bridge carries it across the mouth of the Tavy. Only the size of this bridge hints at the line's former importance.

The route is now inland, broadly following the Tavy to Bere Ferrers, with more enjoyable views out over the river. The station here appears to be in some sort of timewarp. The fine buildings stand in good condition, complete with signal box and goods shed, and freely scattered over them are old signs advertising forgotten products and enamel name boards. There are even milk churns on the platform, awaiting collection by some ghostly local goods train.

The line winds through the hills, climbing steeply through a series of old stone bridges covered in lichen. The Tamar can be seen through the hills, and there is a view down towards Cotehele House, with its own quay on the river. At Bere Alston the train

came to a dead end and several people got off, to disappear into the hinterland. The driver walked along to the other end, taking his time, and then the train set off again the way it had come, shortly branching off to start the slow climb up the old Callington branch. This was a trip into the past, twisting and turning, the wheels screaming and banging on the bends, lineside trees and flowers almost within reach, branch line life as it used to be. The wide, curving river Tamar came into view again, and the train turned slowly on to the great viaduct, its 15mph speed perfect for a leisurely appreciation of the wonderful view from the top of the high arches, with the boats at Calstock far below. The viaduct, 117 feet above the river and over 300 yards long, is a splendid structure, its scale and grandeur quite disproportionate to the minor line it carries. It was built in 1908 by the ambitiously named, but not very important, Plymouth, Devonport & South Western Junction Railway, and is remarkable for its pioneering use of concrete blocks for its structure. It is wonderfully placed in the landscape, its twelve tall narrow arches striding across the valley, the last of all those great railway viaducts. At Calstock station a couple got off to walk down to Cotehele, the guard having given them directions.

This is the high point of the journey, but there is more to come. A minor level crossing causes the train to stop and hoot before cautiously proceeding on its way, and then there is another fine view, down to Morwellham Quay in the valley below. Suddenly the landscape is entirely Cornish, with the overgrown chimneys of the old mine engine houses all around on the hills, romantic echoes of a Cornwall that had already begun to vanish before the railway age. The train ground its slow way up into the hills and then, without warning, it came to a stop, seemingly in the middle of a field. This was Gunnislake, the end of the line. The few remaining passengers wandered away down the rather inadequate platform. Plans are in hand to make a new station across the road. Nevertheless, it seems a rather arbitrary place to end a journey, a line drawn on a map in a far distant planning office in the early 1960s.

Below *Still painted in its Southern Railway livery, Class 02 0-4-4T No.216 stands at Calstock station with the 4.23pm Callington to Bere Alston train on 21 June 1949*

Opposite *Unrebuilt 'West Country' Class 4-6-2 No.34104* Bere Alston *at Cowley Bridge Junction with a Plymouth to Waterloo express on 9 June 1960*

Below *5700 Class 0-6-0PT's Nos.4610 and 4694 bank a heavy bulk cement train out of Exeter St David's station up the heavily graded incline to Central station on 1 September 1964*

Exeter to Barnstaple

Standing on the platform at Exeter St David's station, it is possible to watch trains for London departing in opposite directions. This delightful incongruity is a legacy of the old days of the Great Western and the London & South Western, later the Southern Railway, competing companies whose West Country trains met at Exeter. Today, the InterCity 125s, the modern equivalent, up to a point, of the classic GWR green locomotives and cream and brown carriages, set off eastwards towards Paddington via Taunton. The South Western turbo trains which have taken on the mantle of the Southern's slab-sided locomotives and green carriages, set off westwards and then climb the steep gradient up to Exeter Central, curving round to start the rather slower journey to Waterloo via Salisbury. This pleasant journey, along a pretty route that nearly closed, is famous for a number of lasts. It was the last regular

steam-hauled service out of Waterloo in the 1960s; more recently it was the last line in Britain to see those elderly Class 50 diesels with classic names such as *Indefatigable, Indomitable, Repulse, Bulwark* and *Sir Edward Elgar*; and finally it witnessed the last days of regular locomotive haulage of any kind out of Waterloo.

St David's is still a good station, with many echoes of its complicated past. The classical façade sets the scene. Built in 1864, and redeveloped in 1911, it gives the station, when seen from the distance across the valley, the look of a grand country house. Inside there is a range of 1930s ceramic direction markers in GWR brown, including some fine pointing fingers. The old panelled waiting room has recently been modernised, and spoiled, but at least it has kept its collection of 1950s black and white views of West Country resorts. There are still trains to surprising places, such as Liverpool and Aberdeen, while rumbling freight locomotives hint at various old-time activities. Even more surprising, and linked to a far more distant past, is a series of neo-classical murals lining the stairs to the overbridge. Painted recently by Bridget Green, these show modern travellers in splendidly baroque settings. A brass plaque offers 'Special thanks to Michelangelo Buonarroti whose original work in the Sistine Chapel inspired these designs'.

The 08.56 from Exeter St David's to Barnstaple is, inevitably, a Sprinter in familiar Regional Railways livery, and the departure with its ten passengers is unobtrusive. St David's is well away from Exeter's centre, and so the route along the Exe Valley is immediately out into the rich tones of green that distinguish this journey. At Cowley Bridge Junction the train swings northwards, away from the old Great Western main line, and this marks the beginning of what British Rail's marketing wizards have called the Tarka Line. With Henry Williamson's popularity being far from its zenith, there must be many travellers on this line who have no idea who or what Tarka was. Children can claim their Tarka Line adventure packs, which explain all, and give them so much to do that they never have time to look out of the window, and so miss the

Above *Exeter to Barnstaple Sprinter departs from Crediton station in June 1993*

famous West Country holiday name. To anyone brought up in southern England in the 1950s with even a distant interest in trains, all these names are familiar because they had locomotives named after them, the chunky Pacifics of Southern's 'West Country' class. And for anyone who was actually a train spotter, that litany of names is still unforgettable, *Bude, Bideford, Crediton, Crewkerne, Okehampton, Taw Valley* (a rare survivor today) . . .

Crediton is still a station with presence, its buildings dating back to 1851, when it was the terminus of the Exeter & Crediton Railway. At that time this little company was briefly in the pocket of the Great Western, and so the station, controlled from 1862 by the rival LSWR and subsequently by the Southern, still hints at the hand of Brunel. A family got on, complete with picnic, setting off on their half-term outing undeterred by the steady rain. Nearby, golfers were also ignoring the heavy skies. The only person who seemed unaware of the weather was the guard, unseasonably dressed in a short-sleeved shirt, and resolutely cheerful.

At Crediton the driver collected a token for the single-tracked section ahead, the signalman running out through the rain to hand it over, and then the train rattled on to Yeoford, a ghost station of empty and disused platforms, the meagre remains of a once busy junction. From here trains went northwards to Bideford, Barnstaple and Ilfracombe, or, after a few miles, branched westwards to Plymouth, Bude and Padstow. Nearly all of this network, built so laboriously between the 1850s and the 1890s, has disappeared, leaving only the branch northwards to Barnstaple and a short section westwards to Okehampton, which is used solely as a freight line for trains from Meldon Quarry (a major source of rail ballast). It is on this line that there survives, precariously, the famous Meldon viaduct, a spidery wrought-iron structure of 1874, high above a wooded gorge and looking like something out of North America. There is now nothing quite like it in Britain.

The train ran on through Copplestone and Morchard Road, no one wanting to get on or off. Each station has a big yard, overgrown and abandoned, clues to the essential role played by the

Tarka landscape completely. Adults have to rely on distant memories, or their imagination.

The train galloped along through vast green fields, with only the generous, multi-arched bridges to indicate that this rural route was once the old Southern Railway's main line from London to the West Country. In the days of steam, this was the route for the Atlantic Coast Express, from Waterloo to Exeter, which it entered, confusingly, from the west and then set off again, even more confusingly, eastwards to Ilfracombe, Bude and Padstow, resorts that are redolent with the great days of British holidaymaking.

Today, this route is just a branch line to Barnstaple, much of it single-tracked and many of the stations request stops only. The guard had dutifully explained the procedure for those wishing to get off at such a station. The first real or, in British Rail-speak, 'station stop' is Crediton, another

railway in the local economy. One can imagine those yards filled with wagons loading milk, agricultural produce and cattle for market, a vital backbone to the farms spread over the hills and hidden in the river valleys. That was a true market economy, when, however remote, the station was the centre of its community, the vital link with the world outside.

At Lapford, famous for the Ambrosia dried milk factory which closed in 1970, there is a fertiliser depot, a recent tenuous connection with the railway's agricultural past. Fertilisers in bulk are virtually the only farm cargo still carried by rail but only the rusting siding remains as a memory of this service to Lapford which ceased in 1991. But the huge mountains of white plastic sacks are a depressing reminder that farming is now just another multi-national industry driven by principles of short-term gain. More appealing is the station name laid out in old white bricks. Here, at least, the tradition of railway gardening still lingers on.

This is a journey of rivers, from the Exe to the Taw, via the Yeo, and soon after Lapford the train enters the Taw Valley, following the river closely to its estuary. It is the Taw that was the inspiration behind the name given to this railway, the Tarka Line, and from Eggesford to Barnstaple the route is part of the 180-mile Tarka Trail, a wander through the Devon hills, valleys and woodland that were home to Williamson's famous otter.

At Eggesford the family with the picnic got off and marched into the surrounding woodland determined to enjoy the walks and trails laid out by the Forestry Commission, despite the rain that by now was clearly set in for the day. The guard also got off to operate the level crossing, drawing his orange anorak over the sharply ironed creases of his short-sleeved shirt. The journey continued beside the river, meandering and fast flowing by turns, with the railway contributing to the landscape with its rough-cut granite bridges. Remote stations slipped by, King's Nympton, Portsmouth Arms and Umberleigh, where the fine original North Devon Railway buildings are now a house. Another station now in domestic use is Chapelton, complete with pretty canopy and old SR green enamel station name.

Below *The up Devon Belle Pullman train near Crediton on 28 August 1954 behind unrebuilt 'Battle of Britain' Class 4-6-2 No.34058 Sir Frederick Pile*

Left *Barnstaple to Exeter Sprinter passes Eggesford Church in June 1993*

Right *4300 Class 2-6-0 No.6363 on the turntable at Barnstaple Junction shed before working a train to Taunton via Dulverton on 20 July 1964*

As the line approaches Barnstaple, the river widens, the hills recede and the train races towards the town, spread out along the horizon and marked by its big church. On the right are the remains of the former Great Western line from Taunton via Dulverton, a Beeching victim. The end of the line came abruptly at a set of buffers in a big stone station. The dereliction of its empty and disused platforms is softened by some careful gardening, while the overgrown tracks of long-closed lines stretch ahead into the distance. This was formerly Barnstaple Junction, the meeting point of trains for Ilfracombe via the far more central Barnstaple Town station, for Bideford, Torrington and southwards to Halwill Junction and beyond, and for Great Western services to Taunton via Dulverton. In the early 1960s there were still several trains a day from Waterloo to Barnstaple and Ilfracombe. Until 1935, Barnstaple also had its own narrow gauge railway, the Lynton & Barnstaple, which opened at the end of the nineteenth century to cater for the growing tourist traffic. It boasted, at Chelfham, the largest viaduct on any British narrow gauge line.

Right *End of the line at Barnstaple station, now a ghost of its former self*

Today Barnstaple is a sad station, a long way from the town and surrounded by decay and the ghosts of a glorious past. Its daily ration of Sprinters come and go maintaining a link, via Exeter, between the Exmouth and Barnstaple branch lines. They rarely stay long, but they continue to make accessible the remote villages and farms, and the lovely soft landscape, of the Taw Valley. Those wishing to see more can hire a Tarka Trail bicycle at the station.

The Atlantic Coast Express
Nothing is more simply evocative of the great days of railway travel than famous named trains. Any pre-1960 timetable is full of such trains whose names alone are enough to bring to life the vision of an express pounding through the landscape.

The great named expresses that served the West Country were the Cornish Riviera and the Atlantic Coast, the former from Paddington, the latter from Waterloo. The Atlantic Coast Express was the Southern Railway's flagship during the inter-war years, probably even more famous than the Belles to Brighton and Bournemouth or the Southampton boat trains, and it remained in the British Railways timetable well into the 1960s. Perhaps the greatest of all Britain's holiday trains, it was certainly the most complex. On a busy summer Saturday in the 1950s, Waterloo would witness the departure of a succession of trains called the Atlantic Coast Express, all fully equipped with restaurant cars, and all serving different destinations. All raced to Salisbury, where there was a high-speed change of locomotive, and then onwards to Exeter, some having left behind a section of coaches that would go on to other West Country resorts in a more leisurely manner. From Exeter the expresses fanned out, with through coaches or even whole trains going to Barnstaple and Ilfracombe, Bideford and Torrington, or Okehampton, Bude and Padstow. As these so-called 'portmanteau' expresses were made up of coaches for a variety of destinations, it was always important for passengers to get into the correct part of their particular Atlantic Coast Express.

The romance lived on into the early 1960s, when every summer Saturday two Atlantic Coast Expresses were leaving Waterloo, at 10.35am for Bude and Padstow, and at 11.00am for Barnstaple, Torrington and Ilfracombe. And these were supported by a series of other, un-named West Country restaurant car expresses. Within a few years, however, all had gone – not just the trains themselves, but the destinations they served, victims of some of the most violent swings of the Beeching axe. Paddington was left in complete control of the West Country.

The Conwy Valley Line

Llandudno Junction to Blaenau Ffestiniog

FOR A STATION with no town to serve, Llandudno Junction is surprisingly grand, with plenty of handsome redbrick buildings still surviving and long platforms which dwarf the Sprinters that are its most frequent visitors. There is a pleasantly old-fashioned buffet, whose halls are decorated with large photographs of famous steam locomotives taken during visits to the station while hauling recent specials. And there is a curious box-like waiting room, with a public telephone so placed that everyone in the room has no choice but to listen to every word of any call. The comings and goings of trains, both local and long-distance, add interest, along with some still-active freight sidings. Seemingly in the middle of nowhere, the station is in fact only just across the river from Conwy, and it retains its junction status thanks to the rather unexpected survival of the two branch lines that made it a junction in the first place. One of these is the short link north to Llandudno via Deganwy. In its day this was a major holiday route, terminating in a huge station that today looks sadly decayed and under-used. The other line, branching away to the south, is the old London & North Western route that climbs into the mountains, following the twists and turns of the rivers Conwy and Lledr on its way to Blaenau Ffestiniog.

The 16.06 from Llandudno Junction to Blaenau was a single car Sprinter, holding its predictable complement of elderly couples with shopping bags and young girls with personal stereos, augmented on this occasion by a group of walkers with big

Llandudno to Blaenau Ffestiniog Sprinter pauses at North Llanwrst signal box as the driver exchanges the single-line token with the signalman

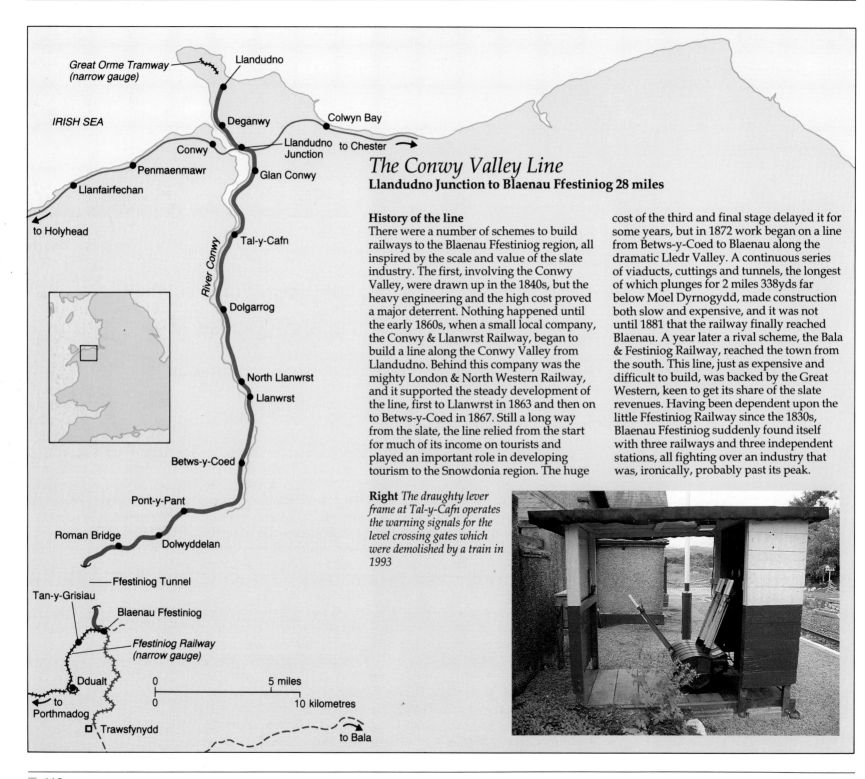

Great Orme Tramway
(narrow gauge)

Llandudno

IRISH SEA

Deganwy

Colwyn Bay

Conwy

Llandudno
Junction

to Chester

Penmaenmawr

Glan Conwy

Llanfairfechan

to Holyhead

River Conwy

Tal-y-Cafn

Dolgarrog

North Llanwrst

Llanwrst

Betws-y-Coed

Pont-y-Pant

Roman Bridge

Dolwyddelan

Ffestiniog Tunnel

Tan-y-Grisiau

Blaenau Ffestiniog

Ffestiniog Railway
(narrow gauge)

Ddualt

to
Porthmadog

Trawsfynydd

0   5 miles
0   10 kilometres

to Bala

The Conwy Valley Line
Llandudno Junction to Blaenau Ffestiniog 28 miles

History of the line

There were a number of schemes to build railways to the Blaenau Ffestiniog region, all inspired by the scale and value of the slate industry. The first, involving the Conwy Valley, were drawn up in the 1840s, but the heavy engineering and the high cost proved a major deterrent. Nothing happened until the early 1860s, when a small local company, the Conwy & Llanwrst Railway, began to build a line along the Conwy Valley from Llandudno. Behind this company was the mighty London & North Western Railway, and it supported the steady development of the line, first to Llanwrst in 1863 and then on to Betws-y-Coed in 1867. Still a long way from the slate, the line relied from the start for much of its income on tourists and played an important role in developing tourism to the Snowdonia region. The huge cost of the third and final stage delayed it for some years, but in 1872 work began on a line from Betws-y-Coed to Blaenau along the dramatic Lledr Valley. A continuous series of viaducts, cuttings and tunnels, the longest of which plunges for 2 miles 338yds far below Moel Dyrnogydd, made construction both slow and expensive, and it was not until 1881 that the railway finally reached Blaenau. A year later a rival scheme, the Bala & Festiniog Railway, reached the town from the south. This line, just as expensive and difficult to build, was backed by the Great Western, keen to get its share of the slate revenues. Having been dependent upon the little Ffestiniog Railway since the 1830s, Blaenau Ffestiniog suddenly found itself with three railways and three independent stations, all fighting over an industry that was, ironically, probably past its peak.

Right *The draughty lever frame at Tal-y-Cafn operates the warning signals for the level crossing gates which were demolished by a train in 1993*

boots and even bigger rucksacks, and an American couple on their way to catch the narrow gauge Ffestiniog Railway's last steam train of the day, the 17.15 from Blaenau to Porthmadog. The Americans spent much of the journey reading out to each other excerpts from a Ffestiniog brochure, exclaiming at the pictures and speculating about which locomotive they would be hauled by. Curiously, it was the rather large lady who showed the greater interest, while her tall, balding and bespectacled partner was only just managing to keep his boredom at bay.

Roaring lustily, in typical fashion, the Sprinter slid out of the station, clattered over the points and set off up the Conwy Valley. After a mile or so of industrial clutter, the route was immediately attractive, the train running along the river's eastern bank with a magnificent view back over the estuary and the dramatic skyline of Conwy Castle. It was recognisably the view painted in the eighteenth century by the pioneering landscape artist, Richard Wilson, and the lack of the picturesque drama supplied then by his Italianate imagination was amply made up for by the Victorian splendour of Stephenson's tubular railway bridge. The Americans, engrossed in a discussion about the Ffestiniog's double-ended Fairlie locomotives, missed the view completely. Having done her ticket rounds, the lady guard returned to her quarters, and then made only an occasional appearance.

The scenic qualities of the Conwy Valley have long been appreciated. Edmund Burke thought it 'the most charming spot in North Wales', and from its early days the route's tourist potential was exploited by the railway, well aware of the valley's appeal as 'a favourite haunt of the angler and the artist'. As early as the 1870s, special open-topped excursion coaches were being used on the line, and from 1913 observation cars were regularly attached to trains during the season. Amazingly, these continued to be used until their final retirement in 1956. Even today one survives, on the preserved Bluebell Railway in Sussex.

However, it was industry rather than tourism that inspired the creation of the Conwy Valley line. In the middle of the eighteenth century, slate

quarrying began in the hills around Blaenau, at the head of the Vale of Ffestiniog, with the slate being laboriously carted down the hills to quays built on the tidal estuary of the river Dwyryd. Despite the difficult nature of the terrain, this industry grew rapidly, thanks largely to the efforts of William Alexander Madocks, who began a process of reclamation of the marshy estuary, built embankments and horse-drawn tramways and, in 1821, planned a new harbour expressly for the shipping of slate. Named Portmadoc (now Porthmadog), this was in operation by 1824, and a new town rapidly developed around it. Madocks then turned his attention to the overland part of the journey and, after a considerable battle, received in 1832 parliamentary assent for a 13^1/4 mile tramway from Blaenau to his new harbour. The Ffestiniog Railway opened in 1836, with a route that was

Above *Lonely wooden steps wait for passengers at Glan Conwy station, situated on the east bank of the afon Conwy*

heavily engineered and included at least one inclined plane. Loaded slate wagons were sent down by gravity and then hauled back empty by horses. It was a time-consuming process, and tunnels were therefore built to replace the inclined plane. As a result, the railway had, by 1851, the route that was to survive for the next century. At the Blaenau end a vast network of quarry railways was built and by the 1860s production of slate had risen to 90,000 tons per year, with 2,000 men employed in the quarries. In the early 1860s the Ffestiniog's engineer, Charles Euston Spooner, introduced steam haulage to speed up operations, the first two locomotives arriving in 1863. An immediate success, this led directly to the start of passenger services on the line in 1865. The continued growth of the slate industry resulted in a need for bigger trains and more powerful locomotives, and so the first of the famous double-boilered Fairlie engines, *Little Wonder*, went into service in 1869. These extraordinary two-ended machines have been the Ffestiniog's trademark ever since. In that same year, the railway carried over 125,000 tons of slate down from the quarries to Porthmadog.

The scale and value of this traffic inevitably attracted the attention of larger, and more rapacious, railway companies and from the 1840s there were a number of schemes to open new routes to Blaenau. The London & North Western was the first, mounting its attack from the north with a series of plans for lines into the hills along the Conwy Valley. Some twenty years later, the Great Western backed an approach from the south, starting from their Vale of Llangollen line at Bala.

The LNWR's attack proved the most serious. Its protégé, the Conwy & Llanrwst Railway, completed its line to Llanrwst in 1863 and in 1867 this was extended to Betws-y-Coed. Popular from the outset with tourists, this line was still a long way from the main source of its inspiration, the slate quarries, and so in 1872 work began on a line from Betws to Blaenau, along the Lledr Valley. Planned originally as a narrow gauge line, this was finally built to standard gauge. It proved to be immensely expensive, involving the construction of seventeen bridges, a major seven-arch rough stone viaduct at Cethyn's Bridge and five tunnels. Of these, the major one was bored for 3,861yds far beneath Moel Dyrnogydd, raised the railway to a height of 790ft above sea level, and took years to complete. The railway was finally opened to its Blaenau terminus in 1881.

A year later the Bala & Festiniog Railway's line from the south arrived, backed by the Great Western. This was nearly as expensive to build, having climbed for twenty-two miles up the Tryweryn Valley from Bala to a summit of 1,278ft above sea level via sixteen viaducts. At Ffestiniog it met, and rebuilt to standard gauge, an existing 3-mile narrow gauge line to Blaenau. Thus, by 1882 Blaenau had both LNWR and GWR stations, each linked to the Ffestiniog but, perversely, with no direct connection between them. Matters remained

Below *During the 1960s this sad scene was repeated many times on British Railways. The guard waves away the last passenger train from Blaenau Ffestiniog to Bala on 4 January 1960*

like this until 1961, with the two stations by then being known as Blaenau North and Blaenau Central. In that year the former GWR line was closed, as part of its route was due to disappear beneath the waters of a new reservoir in the Tryweryn Valley. All that remained was the section from Blaenau to Trawsfynydd, retained to serve the nuclear power station which was being built there. Ironically, in 1964 the two Blaenau stations were finally connected by rail so that the nuclear trains could travel via the Conwy Valley line. Since then, the power station has, in effect, kept open a railway that has always been expensive to maintain and operate. Now that Trawsfynydd is being decommissioned, the line faces a very uncertain future.

Following the big sweeping bends of the Conwy, the Sprinter ground its way up into the valley, its engine labouring on a continuous climb that must have posed a real challenge for a steam locomotive with a heavily laden train. It is a beautiful landscape, sweeping green hills broken by scattered woodland, the intricate pattern of old hedges and isolated white houses. The minor stations are request stops and the train rattled past Glan Conwy and Tal-y-Cafn, no one wanting them. Inside the train, silence reigned, with everyone either asleep or looking out of the windows. There was a brief pause at Dolgarrog, the site of a former junction with a short line built during the First World War to serve the aluminium works and power station across the other side of the valley. Little remains today, of either the railway or the industries it served, the view across the valley showing tall terraces of grey houses set on to the wooded hillsides.

At North Llanrwst the train stopped and a couple got off while the signalman climbed down from his box to hand the driver the token. Until 1989 this was called Llanrwst station, but it was renamed after the opening of a new Llanrwst station nearer the town centre, built for the National Eisteddfod of that year. This new station, just a green painted shelter on a short platform in a cutting, carries a massive slate plaque to commemorate its opening. Three girls, who had

been talking loudly in Welsh all the way, got off here and ran laughing up the slope towards the town, invisible beyond the trees.

The train climbed on up the valley, occasionally crossing the river as it narrowed gradually between the soft green hills on one side and a wooded rocky scarp on the other. After a while, the line entered the trees to run through a lovely canyon of green, with flashes every now and then of the view out over the valley. This continued to Betws-y-Coed, always the centre of the railway's tourist trade. The LNWR opened a hotel here in 1881 and that set the scene for a station entirely geared to the needs of tourists. It is the major station on the line and still has a good range of buildings. There was a considerable exchange of walkers here, all the ones who had come from Llandudno Junction getting off and being replaced by another, apparently identical group. The first lot had not said much and this new lot proved to be just as silent, all either exhausted

Above *A Llandudno to Blaenau Ffestiniog Sprinter departs from the weed-infested North Llanwrst station, winner of the 1992 Anglo-Irish Best Station Competition*

Right *A Blaenau-bound train crosses the afon Conwy south of Llanwrst*

Below *The Pullman camping coach at Betws-y-Coed station on 28 July 1960*

by the labour of carrying such enormous rucksacks, or reduced to silence by the Americans who had continued their dialogue in New York tones, mainly discussing the qualities of the Ffestiniog and its locomotives, but occasionally digressing on to other Welsh narrow gauge lines. With her ample figure in its ill-fitting jeans, and her even more ample voice, the lady of the couple certainly filled the carriage. The man played a more supporting role, his softer voice, querulous from time to time, feeding her the sentences, liberally sprinkled with 'honeys', that kept her going. It was an impressive performance.

Betws-y-Coed has more to offer, besides walking. In 1975 a railway museum was opened on the old sidings by the station and this has gradually been expanded to include rolling stock and locomotives, a long 7 1/4in gauge garden railway around the site and a miniature electric tramway. Engrossed by some particularly arcane point, the Americans failed to notice that the garden railway featured small-scale American locomotives. One carriage held a café, doing good business at the end of the day. A long line of elderly rolling stock, mostly goods wagons in need of some loving care and a lick of paint, sat on an isolated stretch of track. Included among them, rather sad and out of place, was an old Pullman. Dating from 1910, this had served out its last years as a very popular camping coach in the station yard here.

The train left Betws-y-Coed behind and turned into the valley of the Lledr. As it did so, the landscape immediately changed to something wilder and more dramatic, the line cutting its way through rocks and woodland. This was the section that cost the LNWR dear with its heavy engineering in the form of a series of tunnels and viaducts. The tunnels and bridges, rocky and primitive-looking, seemed only just large enough for the train, which squeezed through, roaring and hooting. It was as though they were a compromise between the original plan to build the railway as a narrow gauge line, and the final decision to make it standard gauge after all. The most impressive structure is the seven-arched Lledr viaduct, or Cethyn's Bridge, built from large lumps of stone apparently piled up dry, without mortar, and capped with battlements.

This rather primitive style was adopted to suit the traditional quality of the landscape and, although it gives a certain sense of picturesque insecurity, it has stood firm since 1879.

The train seemed to climb ever more steeply, following the twists and turns of the river. It did not stop at Pont-y-Pant, but at Dolwydellan another smaller group of walkers was waiting on the platform. Around the station lay the village, a self-contained community of stone farms and independent-looking terraces of grey houses. High on a hill to the west stood the remains of Dolwyddelan Castle, romantic and gloomy in the evening light, and then there was a brief pause at Roman Bridge station.

More twists and turns followed, ever sharper, and then the train plunged into the long tunnel beneath Moel Dyrnogydd. This seemed interminable, its length somehow increased by the proximity of the rough-hewn stone walls that

Above *The 7¹/₄in gauge Denver & Rio Grande train awaits departure from the Conwy Valley Railway Museum at Betws-y-Coed*

Left *The spectacular Pont Gethin viaduct carries the Conwy line over the afon Lledr*

Right *A panoramic view of Blaenau Ffestiniog and its slate workings circa 1885. The GWR station can be seen on the left and the Newborough slate mill in the foreground*

looked as though they would brush the carriage sides. At some point during this subterranean journey, the lady guard emerged and tried to discuss some ticketing matter with one of the passengers, but the noise was so great that neither of them understood a word the other said, and so, after a session of smiling and nodding, she returned to her lair. The train roared on, the noise bouncing to and fro off the rock walls, and then it emerged into the light again, and into a completely different world. Instead of the green walls of the Lledr Valley, there was a landscape composed entirely of mountains and broken grey slate, monochrome,

towering up towards the grey sky. The line seemed to have been carved out of this gigantic pile of broken slate, winding its way through a deep valley formed over a century and a half by the slate industry. These were the waste-tips, and rising up them were the precipitous slopes of the old cable-worked inclined planes and the steep zig-zags of the workers' paths. At higher levels were platforms, the remains of old buildings and the immovable debris of this industry that was really the child of the railways. Sixty years ago this was a hive of activity, with miles of narrow gauge railway to draw the hewn slate from underground caverns

Above *A Llandudno to Blaenau Ffestiniog Sprinter rumbles out of the 2 mile 338yd long Ffestiniog tunnel surrounded by the ghostly remains of the slate industry*

town and a countryside filled with ghosts. The tourist industry has moved in, and slate workings and slate caverns have been re-opened as part of the Great British Theme Park Experience. Souvenir shops sell unlikely objects made from slate. Meanwhile, Blaenau struggles on, a town that has been dying for years, lingering on after the death of the industry that kept it going, and inevitably a rather sad place, despite the grants from the EEC and despite the artificial life injected into it by the tourist invasion.

The train worked its way through the slate landscape, scattering the sheep, and drifted into the town, passing first the remains of the old LNWR station and sidings. It then came to rest in the new joint British Rail and Ffestiniog station, whose creation in 1983 represented a triumph for the volunteers and enthusiasts who had rescued the line. Waiting at its platform was the long line of squat red carriages, filled with expectant faces, and in the distance, smoke and steam rose from the twin funnels of the Fairlie locomotive. The Sprinter's driver cut his engine, and walked away to have his tea. The passengers walked up from the platform, some to disappear into Blaenau's empty streets, and the rest to cross the footbridge to the Ffestiniog platform, led by the American couple, still deep in discussion, their voices now raised in excitement. When everyone had found a seat, the guard, in pale grey three-piece suit and with a flower in his buttonhole, walked the length of the train locking the doors. The locomotive whistled, the lady fireman clambered into the central cab, and the driver eased his train out of the station. The plume of smoke marked its route through the town, out into the valley and past the lake before it disappeared on its way to Porthmadog, a train that is both an enthusiast's dream and, unusually in the present world, a social necessity and a vital link between two outposts of the British Rail network. If privatisation kills the Conwy Valley line, then all those years of struggle that brought the Ffestiniog back to life will have been wasted. Now it is a real railway. Deprived of its British Rail connections, it will become just another tourist fantasy, going nowhere in particular.

to the workshops and to transport the finished product down into the valley and to the freight yards of the Blaenau's three railways, the LNWR, the GWR and the Ffestiniog. The waste was simply poured down the slopes, creating a landscape of grey wilderness that, in the sunshine, has an extraordinary and unexpected beauty. Everything is made of slate, the walls, the houses, the gateposts, even the tombstones, the ever present legacy of an industry whose great years in the late nineteenth century turned Blaenau into a flourishing town and Porthmadog into a major international port.

Today, there is just a landscape of slate, and a

Slate and the Ffestiniog Railway

The hills and mountains of North Wales contain huge deposits of slate, the serious exploitaion of which began in the eighteenth century. Quarries and mines were initially slow to develop because of the problems of transporting the slate across the difficult terrain, but this all changed in the early nineteeenth century with the opening up of extensive horse-drawn tramway networks. As a bulk product, worked slate had to be transported by sea, and the growth of the industry was therefore dependent upon the availability of suitable ports. As these did not already exist, they were created, notably Port Dinorwic, on the Menai Strait and Portmadoc, on the estuaries of the Dwyryd and the Glaslyn. From these, tramway links were gradually driven into the surrounding hills to give direct access to the quarries. A key figure in the development of the slate industry was William Alexander Madocks. It was he who reclaimed the Dwyryd estuary, built the new harbour at Portmadoc and its associated town from 1821, and began the construction, in 1832, of a 13¼-mile tramway to link Portmadoc with the huge slate deposits at Blaenau Ffestiniog. This, the Ffestiniog Railway, opened in 1836. The line descended steadily all the way, and for nearly twenty years loaded wagons were sent down to Portmadoc by gravity, with horses pulling the empty wagons back up to the quarries. It was a complicated line, with an inclined plane that was later replaced by a tunnel. By the early 1860s it was carrying up to 90,000 tons of slate per year. In 1863 steam haulage was introduced, making the Ffestiniog the backbone of an extensive network of quarry railways, all built to narrow gauge. Steam haulage also made possible the start of passenger carrying, in 1865. Successful and independent, the Festiniog Railway Company was fully equipped and its works at Boston Lodge was able to build and maintain rolling stock and locomotives. A characteristic of the company was its development of the Fairlie patent double-boilered locomotive, and a number of these two-ended machines with their central cab were brought into service from 1869.

International competition brought a rapid decline in the slate industry during the early decades of the twentieth century, resulting in a steady closure of both quarries and their railway networks. The Ffestiniog managed to keep going, relying increasingly on the tourist trade, but its decline was inexorable and by the Second World War it was derelict. Enthusiasts mounted a rescue of the line in 1954 and brought the Ffestiniog slowly back to life. Since then the Festiniog Railway Society, manned largely by enthusiasts and volunteers, has reopened the whole line to Blaenau Ffestiniog, a major operation including the creation of a new stretch of line complete with spiral and tunnel to replace the original route flooded by a hydro-electric scheme. The most important of all the Welsh narrow gauge lines, the Ffestiniog offers a proper all-year service and, thanks to its British Rail connections at both Porthmadog and Blaenau Ffestiniog, its route is an important link that fulfills local and tourist needs.

Below *Ffestiniog Railway 0-4-0 No.4* Palmerston, *built in 1864, departs from Porthmadog Harbour Station with a train for Minffordd on 5 September 1993*

The Cambrian Coast Line

Machynlleth to Pwllheli

A STRANGELY ill-assorted group waits on the platform at Machynlleth for the 10.30 train to Pwllheli. An elderly couple stand with a little girl, obviously their grand-daughter, whose arms are tightly wrapped round an enormous yellow teddy bear. Beside them is a lad with a noisy Walkman and a blank expression. A little way away an old man in a raincoat and muffler reads a map intently, and nearby on a bench a young couple sit bickering fiercely. The train is in a siding outside the station, by the old engine shed, its engines idling. It is a cold and windswept day, and no one seems inclined to pass the time by examining the station, a building of considerable charm and architectural interest, whose rustic stonework and steep gables with decorative bargeboarding give it the air of an enlarged Victorian cottage. Dating from 1863, it is a bold and proudly independent style statement by its makers, the little Newtown & Machynlleth Railway.

Soon, the two men seated in the driving compartment break off their conversation and one of them, with some reluctance, revs up the engines and slowly brings the train into the platform, its two coaches unexpectedly bearing the bright green livery of the Birmingham Centro network. After a short delay the doors open and everyone gets into the rearmost coach. The little girl shows her teddy bear various things out of the window and the young couple continue to bicker. Finally the doors close and the train sets off, out along the valley of the Dyfi. It is a rich green landscape, trees set against a background of hills. As the valley widens,

With Cader Idris in the background, a Shrewsbury to Pwllheli train approaches Barmouth soon after crossing the afon Mawddach on the spectacular Barmouth Bridge

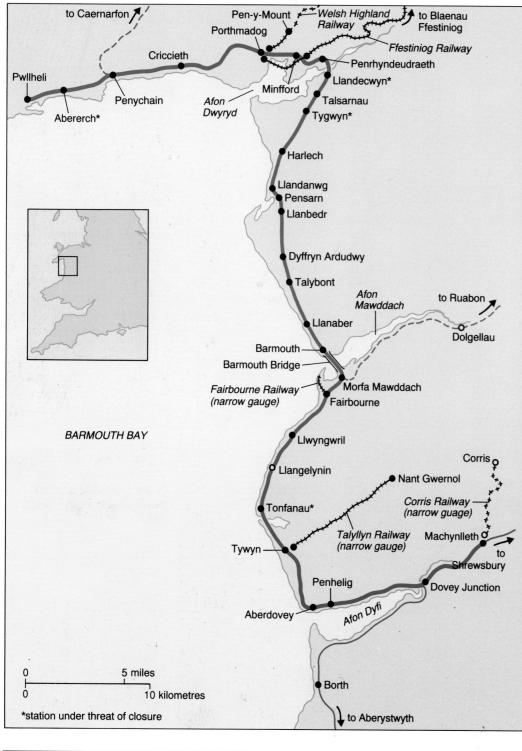

BARMOUTH BAY

*station under threat of closure

0 — 5 miles
0 — 10 kilometres

The Cambrian Coast Line
Machynlleth to Pwllheli 57½ miles

History of the line

From the 1840s a number of railway companies had their sights on Aberystwyth and the Cambrian Coast, but many years were to pass before these schemes were completed. Development was initially from the Welsh borders, with a number of small companies, such as the Llanidloes & Newtown and the Oswestry & Newtown, opening up in the 1850s. In 1858 the Newtown & Machynlleth Company began an extension westwards of these routes and this, with its heavy engineering, was completed in 1863. The same year many of these small companies were merged, to form Cambrian Railways. The next year saw the completion of the line from Machynlleth to Aberystwyth and the start of the gradual opening up of a line northwards along the Cambrian Coast. Progress was slow, hindered by the difficulties of crossing the various estuaries along the route, notably the Mawddach at Barmouth, but the line was finally opened to Pwllheli in 1867. At the same time, the London & North Western Railway had inspired the building of a line from Bangor southwards to Caernarfon and on to Pwllheli, meeting the Cambrian Railways line at Afonwen and making accessible by rail all of northwest Wales. Increasingly successful through the last years of the nineteenth century, these routes benefited directly from the growth of the holiday traffic. The lines were taken over in 1923 by the Great Western and the LMS respectively and continued to be busy with both freight and passenger traffic, the latter greatly expanded by long-distance through trains from Manchester, Birmingham and London. Notable was the famous Cambrian Coast Express from Paddington, which continued to run until the 1960s. With the closure in the 1960s of the linking lines, from the north through Caernarfon, east to Wrexham via Llangollen, Corwen, Bala and Barmouth, and south from Aberystwyth, the Cambrian Coast became little more than a long branch line, living on borrowed time.

the train crosses a huge expanse of watermeadows and marshland, populated by sheep, cows and wild-looking ponies. With wheels squealing and clattering, it runs into Dovey Junction, swinging on to the line that curves away towards the northern shore of the estuary. One old lady waits on the bleak and desolate platform. She climbs into the empty front coach and the train moves off again, crossing immediately the trestle viaduct that carries the railway across the Dyfi. The line to Borth and Aberystwyth can be seen running along the southern shore and away towards the terminus in Aberystwyth's once-grand but now little-used 1920s station.

The Cambrian Coast line is a strangely isolated railway today, having lost in the 1960s and 1970s all the connections that had kept it busy in the past. Gone are the lines southwards from Aberystwyth to Carmarthen, eastwards from Barmouth to Dolgellau and Bala, and northwards from Afonwen, near Criccieth, to Caernarfon and Bangor. Now the only way on to it is via Dovey Junction, on the heavily engineered and rather spectacular line from Shrewsbury that winds its way in between the mountains of Central Wales. Its only regular traffic are the diesels making their way

Above *A Cambrian Railways 2-4-0 and its train of four-wheeled carriages poses with railway staff at Machynlleth station circa 1885*

Left *A Pwllheli to Shrewsbury train cautiously crosses the bridge over the afon Dyfi near the isolated Dovey Junction station. There is no road access to the station which is used by passengers transferring to and from Aberystwyth trains*

Above *A Pwllheli-bound train skirting the Dyfi Estuary at Abertafol, east of Penhelig. Until 1985 a small wooden halt was situated here*

up and down the coast on the two branch lines from Machynlleth. Even the most hardened enthusiast has to admit that it is something of a miracle that there are railways still running along the west coast of Wales.

Flanking the estuary, the line wends its way towards the sea. The guard makes his tour, a stocky young man with an ear-ring and a short pony-tail, dealing smoothly in his lilting Welsh voice with the various ticket requirements and the anxious queries of his little group of passengers. The old man still stares intently at his map, as though certain that the driver has taken the wrong route. Presently, he folds it up and puts it away, and spends the rest of the journey with a resigned look on his face. The girl of the bickering couple, now silent and sitting several seats apart, asks how long until her station. The answer is in hours. She looks depressed. Her partner has put on his Walkman, and looks resolutely away from her when she tries to speak.

The train travels along beside the sea, its route just above the vast stretch of sand exposed by the falling tide, and then in and out of clumps of trees and through rocky outcrops in cuttings and short tunnels. The wheels squeal and the lineside bushes reach out to brush the coaches. In little hidden coves, old boats have been pulled up on the rocks and left to die. A horizon of hills fades into the grey southern distance. At Penhelig the train pauses at a platform of old wooden sleepers, set high above the little harbour. A woman with a shopping bag gets into the first coach, and starts talking to the solitary old lady from Dovey Junction. Rocks give way to dunes and a wide expanse of glittering, empty sea and then there is a caravan park, the first of many.

A view of windswept, tussocky grass and patches of sand now spreads towards the horizon. On the other side, tall grey houses with their backs to the hills announce the beginning of Aberdovey, its old hotels filled with the echoes of family holidays of long ago.

A group of six elderly people, smartly dressed

for an outing and laughing together, waits on the platform. The train stands, its doors firmly shut, and then the guard appears, carrying a set of wooden steps, for Aberdovey's platform is rather low. Steps in place, he opens the doors, and then gives his arm to the two ladies in the group. As soon as they are all seated, the little girl with the teddy bear starts up a conversation with them. She is followed by the guard who, having sorted out their tickets, sits down to join them. The train gallops along, passing a seaside golf course with as many cows as golfers on the links. On the other side, a steep hillside cemetery briefly fills the windows, its flat slate tombstones tipping down towards the sea.

The guard walks back to his compartment and, inspired perhaps by all the passengers he now has in his care, announces that the next station is Tywyn. This turns out to be his only announcement of the whole journey. Adjacent to Tywyn is the narrow gauge Talyllyn Railway's Wharf station, filled with archaic and unusual wagons and paraphernalia. At Tywyn a young couple, holding hands but never speaking, and a boy in school

Above *Penhelig halt and tunnel. This typical GWR halt, with its 'pagoda' design, was opened as recently as 1933*

Left *Cambrian Railways goods train at Aberdovey harbour in 1901*

Above *The approach to Friog avalanche shelter seen from the footplate of 'Dukedog' Class 4-4-0-No.9017 on 30 September 1960*

and closing the line for days. Now there is a concrete avalanche shelter to deflect the falling rocks. Between stretches of wonderful isolation the housing estates, chalet parks and caravan sites come thick and fast, indistinguishable in their gloomy monotony and the curse of the Welsh coastline. Beyond them the hills rise towards the sky, patterned with stone-walled little fields. Tonfanau and Llwyngwril flash past, request stops not wanted on this journey. At Llwyngwril tall grey houses face the sea, their terraces interspersed with clusters of elderly bungalows.

The next stop is Fairbourne, where signs tell passengers to change for the Fairbourne miniature railway. The Fairbourne's route is out along a sandy peninsula that points towards Barmouth, whose handsome grey terraces stand on the hillsides across the estuary. A surprising number of people pile on to the train, including several ladies with shopping trollies. The line then curves round the town to Morfa Mawddach, formerly Barmouth Junction, where the old route to Wrexham via Bala, Corwen, Llangollen and Ruabon turns away from the overgrown platform.

The development of the railways of the Cambrian Coast was, inevitably, the product of company and territorial rivalry. The first schemes date from the 1840s, but nothing happened until the 1850s when small companies such as the Llanidloes & Newtown began to drive lines into the hilly wilderness of Central Wales, with their eyes on the distant goal of Aberystwyth. This was brought nearer by the Newtown & Machynlleth Railway, who from 1857 began to build its route across Wales via Caersws and the Carno Valley. It was an expensive and difficult route, and its major engineering feature was the 120ft deep cutting through the hard gritstone ridge at Talerddig. Completed in 1863, this was for some time the deepest railway cutting in the world. This route is the only one now in use, and Talerddig's sheer rock walls are still an exciting interlude in a journey through dramatic scenery. In 1863, a number of the smaller Welsh companies merged themselves into Cambrian Railways, partly in order to use their united strength to keep at bay the ever-rapacious

uniform get on. There is quite a buzz of conversation in the coach now, with a preponderance of Birmingham accents. Even the bickering couple, now arguing again, have clear Black Country tones. The elderly group starts a serious discussion about spectacles and their cost.

The train runs on beside miles of empty beaches, with only a solitary figure walking a dog to break the line of the sea. Inland, there are dramatic views up remote valleys into the hills. In places, great piles of boulders hide the sea from view, and protect the line from winter storms. This is a line prone to the effects of wild weather and at times it has been closed by floods, snow and other natural disasters. At Friog, near Llwyngwril, where the track is at the base of the rocky cliffs of Cader Idris, landslides have twice, in 1883 and 1933, swept a locomotive far out on to the beach, killing the crew

Great Western, who had a clear interest in the Newtown & Machynlleth.

The extension of the line from Machynlleth to Aberystwyth was completed in 1864, having been built by the curiously named Aberystwith & Welch Coast Railway. At the same time, plans were being drawn up by rival companies for an attack on the Cambrian coast from Caernarfon in the north, via Porthmadog. The inspiration for all this activity came largely from the rapidly expanding holiday trade. New hotels were being opened all the time at developing resorts such as Aberystwyth, Borth, Tywyn and Barmouth, and by the mid-1860s trains were running with through coaches between London and the Cambrian coast. The line north from Dovey Junction was built in a rather piecemeal fashion, with a number of short isolated stretches coming into operation before the problems

Above *'Dukedog' Class 4-4-0 No.9017 at Llwyngwril station with a train for Pwllheli on 30 September 1960. This was probably one of its last days in service as the locomotive was withdrawn shortly afterwards. No.9017 is now preserved on the Bluebell Line in Sussex*

Left *Fairbourne Railway 12^{1}/4 in gauge loco* Sherpa *at the railway's terminus opposite Barmouth. Barmouth Bridge, carrying the Cambrian Coast line over the Mawddach estuary, can be seen in the background*

Above *Cambrian Railways train leaves Barmouth and crosses the original wooden bridge over the Mawddach Estuary in 1896. Opened for traffic in 1867, the timber trestle section was reconstructed between 1906 and 1909. The movable section was rebuilt as a swing bridge in 1900. In the 1980s the bridge was temporarily closed due to infestation by a marine worm*

Opposite *A Shrewsbury to Pwllheli train, dwarfed by cliffs, skirts the harbour as it approaches Barmouth*

posed by the Dyfi and Mawddach estuaries could be overcome. The whole route to Pwllheli was finally opened in 1867.

In the early days, this was always a leisurely journey, made even slower by poor time-keeping and inadequate connections, and for some years it was quicker to get to Pwllheli via the North Wales coastline and Caernarfon, or on the Great Western line from Chester and Wrexham, which featured trains such as the Birmingham, Birkenhead & North Wales Express. The Cambrian coast line was much improved during the early years of this century, and from 1923 much of the network came under Great Western control. The 1920s saw the introduction of the famous Cambrian Coast Express, a regular holiday restaurant car service from Paddington to Aberystwyth and Pwllheli, and in one form or another this continued to run until 1967. During the summer of 1961, for example, the

Cambrian Coast Express left Paddington every weekday at 10.10am, reaching Aberystwyth at 4.15pm, and Pwllheli at 6.10pm. The return service left Pwllheli at 7.40am and Aberystwyth at 9.45am, to reach London at 4pm. The route followed was via Banbury, Birmingham, Wolverhampton, Shrewsbury, Newtown and Machynlleth.

By this time Dr Beeching had removed all the links to the Cambrian Coast line itself, and closure notices for Dovey Junction to Pwllheli were posted in 1971. However, a vigorous and well-fought campaign led to the line being reprieved in 1974. The spectre of closure rose again in 1980, when expensive repairs were needed for Barmouth viaduct, but eventually British Rail was persuaded to find somehow the £1½ million necessary to bring the bridge, and the line, back from the dead. Fully modernised, and with every possible economy measure having been taken, the Cambrian Coast

Opposite Aerial view from the castle of Harlech station. A train for Machynlleth has just arrived to pick up a solitary passenger. Until the early 1950s regular cattle auctions were held in the station yard and involved much activity for the railway

line lives on, albeit on borrowed time. Steam-hauled trains and other specials occasionally run along it and it has a very active support group, but these are not likely to have much influence on the economic 'realism' that will follow private ownership. In these circumstances, both the Cambrian Coast and the old main line to Aberystwyth will be at risk, with the real possibility that the only railways still operating in Central Wales will be preserved tourist lines. And these, deprived of their main line connections, will have no real social or practical value. A linear theme park is of little use to someone who relies on a train to take them shopping or on visits to friends and relatives. And a private or preserved railway that does not have a main line link only forces people into that absurd situation of having to go in the car to take a train to nowhere.

Leaving Morfa Mawddach, the train swings into the long approach to the viaduct across the estuary. Opened in 1867 and completely rebuilt in 1906, this is now the only major timber viaduct still in use on the British Rail network. Damaging infestation by marine boring worms closed the bridge in 1981, but since then the timbers have steadily been replaced or stabilised. The views out to sea, up the Mawddach Valley to mountains piled against the sky, and across to Barmouth are spectacular and the train's slow speed means there is time to enjoy them. At the Barmouth end of the viaduct there are two steel spans, one of which formerly swung open to allow the passage of ships. From here there is also a good view of the end of the Fairbourne Railway, with its little carriages sitting among the dunes at the tip of the sandy peninsula it crosses.

The entry to Barmouth is also enjoyable, passing the lifeboat station, beaches and lines of boats in the harbour. The train crosses the town, above its grey stone houses, before it reaches the large and reasonably original station. Here the coaches almost empty and all the familiar people, the girl with the teddy bear, the man with his map, the elderly group, the silent hand-holding couple, wander off into the town, along with the ladies with shopping trollies. Only the bickering couple remains, still silently apart. Young lads with rucksacks climb on,

and the train starts again, out past the derelict sidings and goods yards and along the beach once more. At a bleak seaside halt at Llanaber, another lad gets on and joins his friends. The landscape unrolls steadily, visions of splendour and delight, a broad canvas of grey, green and yellow flashes, interrupted by yet more caravans in predictably unpleasant colours. Talybont station has a new shelter, with a badge proclaiming that it was funded by the EU, and on either side are fields walled with rounded beach stones. Then comes Dyffryn, its battered old wooden shelter still awaiting its grant, and then the train swings inland, away from the sea to Llanbedr, another little halt that no one wants today.

The landscape changes perceptibly, becoming hillier and with more trees. Suddenly, with no warning, Harlech Castle appears, high on its mound above the town, a wonderful sight from the train in the valley far below. The lads with rucksacks get off. One now has a large sketch pad under his arm. The train goes on again, taking a long last look back to Harlech Castle, and eventually it plunges into the hills, cutting a dramatic inland route to Talsarnau, whose tired old station house carries For Sale boards. On the approach to the station there is a view across the estuary to the steeply wooded slopes of the northern shore. Clough Williams-Ellis's dream village of Portmeirion nestles among the trees, its spires and towers breaking the horizon and its soft colours creating, even in the grey light, the intended vision of Italy. It lingers in the mind, a frivolous delight, a romantic folly, among so much upright architecture in grey and white.

Unaware of Portmeirion's charm, the girl from the bickering couple moves away to a different part of the coach. The line runs on, following the estuary to its head, then crosses the river on a smaller trestle viaduct. The peaks of Snowdonia frame the valley, while to the west a large area of saltmarsh is dotted with sheep. Penrhyndeudraeth has a new station shelter, while in a fold of the hills nearby lurks the explosives factory that gave the line so much of its freight traffic, a series of dark, threatening sheds. Following the estuary's northern shore, the train

Above *Lonely Llandecwyn halt, its platform built of wooden sleepers, is now under threat of closure*

Opposite *With the mountains of Snowdonia in the distance, a Shrewsbury to Pwllheli train slowly crosses Pont Briwet over the afon Dwyryd, near Penrhyndeudraeth*

plunges through woods filled with rhododendrons and into rocky cuttings. In this picturesque landscape the bickering couple are briefly reconciled.

The next station is Minffordd. Three people get off, but none of them follows the signs to join the Ffestiniog Railways train, up on a higher level. When it was completed, the Cambrian Coast line burrowed under the already extant Ffestiniog here, and an exchange link between the two was opened in 1872. The train passes the Ffestiniog's sidings and yards, full of elderly wagons and complicated bits of machinery, and then the landscape turns grey, everything coloured by the dust from the quarry beside the line. Porthmadog now lies ahead, and the train rattles round the back of the town, with distant views of the Cob that carries the Ffestiniog across the estuary, and the harbour. There is a long pause at the level crossing, then it slides into the town's still substantial station, passing the start of

the Welsh Highland Railway, a recent addition to Wales's collection of narrow gauge lines. Originally this ran up into Snowdonia, to Beddgelert, with complex lines to surrounding slate lines, but only the first couple of miles from Porthmadog have been reopened. The passengers change again, ladies with shopping bags replacing the departing walkers, some of whom were setting off through the town to the Ffestiniog's harbour station.

Turning its back on the sea, the train runs inland, climbing steadily through woods for a few miles and then dropping back down to the beach, bleak and windblown, for the approach to Criccieth. The little town and harbour look inviting and, from the train, almost as colourful as Portmeirion. Its houses and boats are overshadowed by the great mass of the ruined castle, high on its mound, and flags fly from the ruined towers. The station is set among old, disused platforms, sad reminders of the great days of the Cambrian Coast as a premier holiday line. The train pauses, but no one gets on or off. It is hard now to imagine this station filled with noise and activity as families, with all their baggage, descended from the Cambrian Coast Express a daily sight during the summer in the 1950s. Then, the elegant dark green Manor class locomotive would slowly have hauled its long train out of the station, its exhaust barking with the effort. Today, the train slips away and no one notices.

The line runs on along the beach and through a pattern of fields backed by a dramatic line of hills. At the old junction at Afonwen the track of the long-gone LNWR line northwards to Caernarfon and Bangor can still be seen, and then the huts and the fairground rides of Butlin's fill the landscape. The station, recently rebuilt and now called Butlin's Penychain, was once one of the busiest on the whole line. Today, only the bickering couple gets off, clearly destined for an exciting week, and a crowd of small boys rushes on, shepherded by a number of anxious women laden with bags. They really want to go to Aberystwyth and have got on the wrong train, but the guard tells them not to worry as his train will go the way they want in the end. They relax and hand out the sandwiches and crisps. The Butlin's car parks are full.

The train enters Pwllheli past the harbour and the new yacht marina, with old sidings and the signal box as echoes of the busy terminus that once existed here. Today there is only one platform in use, and the train crawls to a halt. Everyone gets off, and the driver and guard, deep in conversation, disappear to get their tea. The station, its timber painted in green and white, is like a pavilion at the end of a pier, entirely suitable for the end of a seaside line. The station café, lively, full of posters and old photographs of the railways of Wales in better days, is crowded and obviously justifies the awards it has won. However, no one in it seems to be waiting for a train, and there are not many to wait for, in any case. On a notice board there is the closure notice for four Cambrian Coast line stations, but a sticker across it says that objections have been received. The closures are delayed. Like the future of the whole line, everything is in abeyance.

Above *Cambrian Railway days at Porthmadog. The station staff are captured for posterity in the 1890s*

Opposite *Haymaking time. With the spectacular backdrop of Snowdonia, a Shrewsbury-bound train leaves Porthmadog*

Cambrian connections

Connected to the Cambrian Coast line was a series of small, independent narrow gauge railways, notably the Talyllyn, the Corris, the Fairbourne, the Ffestiniog and the Welsh Highland, all of which survive in some form today.

The Talyllyn was opened from 1866 to serve both the slate industry and the needs of local passengers, its narrow gauge route running for seven miles from Tywyn on the Cambrian Coast line to Nant Gwernol, where there was an inclined plane link to the Abergynolwyn slate quarry. Like the other lines of the region, the Talyllyn benefited from the increase of tourism from the 1880s. With the closure of the slate quarry in the late 1940s, the railway lost its main source of income, and it closed in 1950. A year later it was reopened by volunteers, the first railway in Britain to be preserved in this way, and since then it has established itself as one of the premier Welsh narrow gauge lines.

Also inspired by the slate industry was the Corris Railway, an eleven-mile gravity-worked line opened in 1859 to link slate quarries at Corris and Aberllefenni with the recently opened main line at Machynlleth. Steam haulage arrived in 1879 but there was no regular passenger traffic until 1883. From then on there was increased emphasis on tourism, the company operating horse buses and combined tours with the Talyllyn and the Cambrian Coast line. The decline of the slate industry was, however, critical and passenger services ceased in 1931, shortly after the line's takeover by the GWR. Slate traffic continued in a spasmodic way until 1948, when flooding closed the line. Two years later it had largely disappeared, but volunteers have recently opened a railway museum and a short length of track at Corris.

The Fairbourne Railway is a two-mile narrow gauge line, opened in 1890 to carry building materials to Penrhyn Point. Passenger carrying soon started, linked almost entirely to the needs of tourists. In 1916 Narrow Gauge Railways, Bassett-Lowke's company, took the line over, and rebuilt it as a 15in gauge tourist line, making the most of Fairbourne's famous sandy beaches. After a period of closure following the Second World War and several changes of ownership, the line has been fully restored to $12^{1}/_{4}$in gauge.

The Ffestiniog Railway is covered in detail on page 127.

The Welsh Highland Railway originated as the North Wales Narrow Gauge Railways Company in 1877 and was acquired by the Welsh Highland Railway in 1922. In 1934 the WHR was leased by the Ffestiniog Railway. The line ran from Porthmadog to Dinas Junction via Beddgelert but was not a commercial success and finally closed in 1937. In 1973 a preservation group was formed to reopen the line and a short section from Porthmadog is now operating passenger services.

Right *Welsh Highland Railway 2-6-2T* Russell, *built by Hunslet in 1906 for the North Wales Narrow Gauge Railway, in action again at the WHR terminus adjacent to the Cambrian Coast line at Porthmadog*

Below *The heyday of narrow gauge railways in Wales. A Corris Railway 2ft 3in gauge Falcon 0-4-0ST with its magnificent train of bogie carriages waits to depart from Machynlleth station in 1899*

The Far North of Scotland

Inverness to Wick and Thurso

A NUMBER OF PEOPLE had assembled on the platform at Inverness, waiting for the train to Wick and Thurso, but they were not the typical rural railway travellers. There were none of the usual old ladies on the way to visit family or friends, none of the groups of girls returning from shopping trips, and no young mothers with pushchairs. These were serious travellers, standing on their own or in small groups, some armed with rucksacks and sleeping bags, some with fishing rods or gun cases, some with dogs. All carried quite significant picnics, and plenty of wet weather gear, even though the evening sun was still shining warmly on to the platform. A few were equipped in a more unusual way, two people carrying the distinctive black bags that hold personal computers and one mild-looking young man a huge pair of antlers, held nonchalantly under one arm. There were also some very serious long-distance rail buffs, with British Rail style heavy orange anoraks and holdalls bulging with maps and timetables. A couple had mountain bikes, well laden.

The journey to the very north of Britain is exceptional, in every sense. It is by far the most remarkable of all the services operated by Scotrail, and all the more so for being so little-known. Scotland has many classic rail journeys and the two most famous, Fort William to Mallaig and Inverness to Kyle of Lochalsh, are now well-established tourist routes, with busy, and genuinely international, trains. They feature in books and television programmes with monotonous regularity. By comparison, the Wick and Thurso line is a wonderful secret, spectacular in the

A Wick/Thurso to Inverness train pauses at the remote Kinbrace station in the Strath of Kildonan

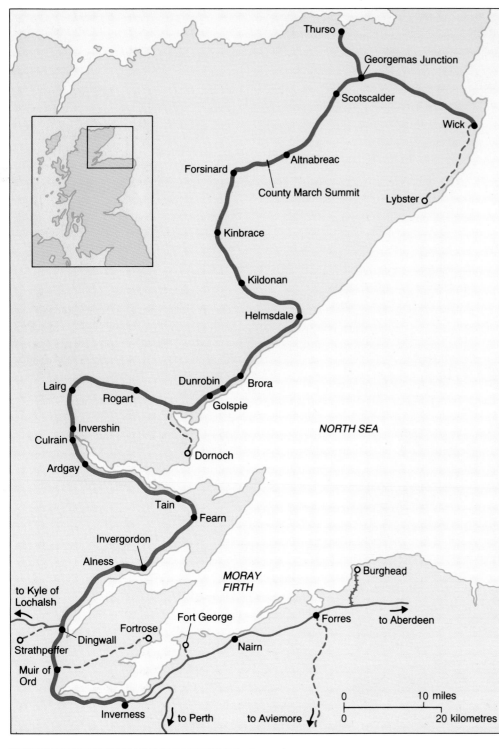

The Far North of Scotland
Inverness to Wick and Thurso 161½ miles

History of the line

The first schemes for a railway to the very north of Britain were drawn up in the early 1860s, inspired largely by the development of Inverness as a centre of railway activity from 1855. Despite the remoteness of the terrain, the small size of the local population and the general lack of industry in the region, the railway went ahead, being built in stages between 1862 and 1874. It had the backing of the local landowners, notably the Duke of Sutherland, who contributed extensively to the construction costs and, indeed, for a number of years was wholly responsible for the building and operation of an entire section of the line, from Golspie to Helmsdale.

Work on the railway began at Inverness, with the first section being built by the Inverness & Ross-shire Company. The line opened to Dingwall in 1862 and to Bonar Bridge in 1864. The Sutherland Railway opened the line to Golspie by 1868 and the Duke of Sutherland's Railway ran up the coast from here. The line was finally completed to Wick and Thurso by the Sutherland & Caithness.

Services were operated by the Highland Railway, who took over the line completely in 1884.

The Wick and Thurso line, despite its apparent lack of potential, proved to be both economically viable and socially useful. Its opening greatly encouraged the growth of established industries such as whisky distilling, engineering, textiles, farming and fishing. Wick and Thurso flourished as centres of herring fishing, and Helmsdale also benefited. The line became the only means of supply for the naval bases at Scapa Flow and Invergordon, and during the First World War its carrying facilities were stretched to the limit. Its social value was also enormous, the railway becoming a lifeline for the small communities of the region. In recent years, the line has been given a new lease of life by the nuclear establishment at Dounreay and by the North Sea oil industry. Ironically, however, their decline now threatens the railway's future which, in the current political climate, has to be seen as insecure.

landscape that surrounds its meandering route and the only truly adventurous rail journey in Britain. The hours that are spent as the train fights its way north are not for the faint-hearted, but the rewards for those who make the effort are all the greater.

Inverness is an interesting station, its rugged origins still pervading the atmosphere. It was built in 1855 by the Inverness & Nairn Railway, but its real importance came later, when it was the hub and controlling centre of the Highland Railway, whose hotel and former offices face each other across the courtyard. It is the distinctive and often dramatic quality of the journeys that begin and end at its platforms that make the station memorable, and the passengers who gather on the generous concourse seem to share a perceptible sense of adventure.

The only disappointment is the train itself. There is nothing epic about the Sprinter and its family derivatives. It is simply a practical means of transport, the best type of genuinely universal, standardised passenger train British Rail has ever produced, but ultimately mundane. The journey to Wick and Thurso has never been the same since the end of locomotive haulage. Steam, of course, finished years ago, but the line was well served by

Left *The interior of the station in Academy Street, Inverness, seen on 27 November 1936*

Above *The cigarette stand, with its wide range of requisites for smokers, at Inverness station in 1927*

generations of growling diesels, the last carriers of the flag being the Class 37s.

The train pulled into the platform, indistinguishable from others of its type, and everyone climbed aboard, spreading themselves throughout the carriages and somehow stowing all their equipment in the somewhat restricted storage space. Much of it, notably rucksacks, fishing bags and the pair of antlers, inevitably went on to spare seats, of which there were quite a few. This was the 18.00, the last of the three weekday services each way on the route. Presently it set off, out of Inverness, spread out behind in the evening light, and along to Clachnaharry, where it rattled over the

1909 swing bridge across the Caledonian Canal, still controlled by a Highland Railway signal box.

It is 717 miles by train from London to Thurso, and those who think that Inverness is in the far north of Scotland should remember that Thurso is another 154 miles on (but rather less as the crow flies, for the route taken by the railway is remarkably indirect). During the latter stages of the First World War, when this line was a vital artery for men and supplies for Scapa Flow and other naval bases at Inverness and Invergordon, there was a daily train for naval personnel from Euston to Thurso, which took 21½ hours. Today, the journey is somewhat quicker, but its epic nature has not been lost. It was from Thurso's harbour that the supply ships sailed for the naval base at Scapa Flow, a tradition maintained today by the ferry service to the Orkneys. A number of people on the train were clearly destined for the ferry, now one of the mainstays of the line.

The train ran west along the shore of the Beauly Firth against a background of grand hills. The guard made his rounds, and then picnics began to appear everywhere, some the usual sandwiches and crisps, others much more ambitious affairs. Two or three families and groups of friends had taken over the seats with tables, liberally spreading them with plates and cutlery, an interesting variety of food and some promising bottles of wine. Soon the carriage had the atmosphere of an informal dining car, with everyone tucking into something and enjoying the view in the soft evening colours.

At the head of the firth, the line swings north to cross the Beauly river, with Beauly town and priory largely hidden by trees. The first stop is at Muir of Ord, formerly a junction for the old branch line along the Black Isle to Fortrose, on the northern shore of the Moray Firth. By the station there is a large grain silo, storing barley for the local whisky distillers. The line then runs on through woodland to cross the river Conon on a large stone viaduct, a typically elegant design by Joseph Mitchell, the engineer of a number of Scottish lines who was trained by Thomas Telford. Skirting the shore at the head of Cromarty Firth, the train reaches Dingwall station, remarkable for its plentiful woodwork and flowers, a handsome awning and a bizarre plaque announcing the extraordinary number of cups of tea supplied to servicemen during the Second World War. Dingwall is also the junction for the line to Kyle of Lochalsh, which turns away to the west just beyond the station. Justly famous, this spectacular route has tended to overshadow its more northerly neighbour, and so benefits from the bulk of the tourist traffic. The Wick and Thurso line seems to appeal more to the seasoned traveller than the tourist, good for those enjoying the route, but not so good for the line's long-term future. Maybe, however, the effects of privatisation north of the border will not be quite so dire as in England and Wales, for Scotrail has been operating more or less as an independent body for years, and will probably benefit from a degree of autonomy and freedom from English decision-making. None the less, the Wick and Thurso line has to be on the endangered list, partly as a result of its serious lack of tourist and freight traffic, and partly because of the way it has suffered at the hands of the road lobby. The curse of the line is the A9 road, recently upgraded at the cost of hundreds of millions and

Below *Dingwall's well-kept station, complete with tea rooms, is the junction for the picturesque route to Kyle of Lochalsh*

including a series of new viaducts that significantly shorten the route. The railway is very much the poor relation, with virtually no share of the cake, despite its potential as a major freight carrier.

An elderly couple got on at Dingwall, complete with sticks, tweeds, serious walking shoes and a pair of labradors who, well-trained, sat quietly under the seats throughout the journey. Climbing, and running initially through a series of cuttings, the train then followed the Cromarty Firth's northern shore, with fine views across to Black Isle. With stations at Foulis and Evanton long closed, the next stop was Alness, a station with a curiously colonial look, and a chequered history. Built in 1863 and closed in 1960, it was reopened in 1973 in response to the oil boom that had brought an unexpected surge of life to the region. Today, the firth around Alness is still full of oil rigs, some in the repair yards, but most mothballed, awaiting for some unlikely event to halt the oil industry's seemingly irreversible decline. Dramatic and colourful, these strange-looking monsters make a significant mark on the landscape, and continue to do so as far as Invergordon. Here the large station hints at the town's complex history. For years a major naval base dominated the scene, notorious for its mutiny during the First World War. Later came whisky distilling, ship repairing, oil drilling and aluminium smelting, all enterprises that have had their ups and downs. The worst was probably aluminium, a huge and heavily subsidised investment that never really got going before it was abandoned in 1981 with the loss of hundreds of local jobs. The gaunt remains of this ill-fated scheme tower beside the railway line, while on the seaward side more old rigs stand as mute reminders of another economic switchback. Whisky lives on, in the form of the huge plants that produce bulk quantities of spirit for blending. A tempting sight are the piles of wooden barrels.

From Invergordon, the train runs northeast along the shore of Nigg Bay, with fine views out over the almost enclosed firth and the narrow jaws that

Right *An elegant Highland Railway cast-iron footbridge at Tain station overlooks the Dornoch Firth*

protect it, and then it turns inland, into an area of woodland, before pausing briefly at Fearn. There seems to be little life left at this station, whose rather formal and curiously domestic-looking buildings went out of railway use some time ago. After Fearn the open views return, ahead to Dornoch Firth and the hills beyond. With the landscape playing such an integral role in the journey, it was refreshing to see most of the passengers actively involved in it. Much of the conversation revolved round things seen through the window. Responses to the piled-up whisky barrels were predictable, but more unexpected was a discussion about the status of religion in the Highlands, inspired by a ruined chapel on a hillside which was surrounded by overgrown graves and wonderfully irregular tombstones. At Tain a number of people got off, drawn perhaps by the elegant appeal of this traditional Highland town, or by the golf, or even by the whisky, for there are several distilleries in the area, notably Glenmorangie, a mile or so outside the town and right beside the railway.

The town of Tain is set on a ridge, above the handsome stone station with its pillared porch. Dornoch Firth stretches ahead, the view nowadays somewhat impeded by the bridge that carries the A9 across the firth. By road it is now no distance across the water to Dornoch, the new bridge saving over twenty miles on the old, indirect inland route along the shores of the Dornoch Firth. When the bridge was being built, Scotrail and many other sensible bodies campaigned for it to carry both road and rail. Economically, the future of the Wick and Thurso line was closely linked to the bridge, but the battle was lost on the usual steeply sloping battleground, with centrally funded and thus unaccountable road building being pushed through regardless of the real cost, while an investment-starved rail system was, as ever, expected to fund a major development out of revenue. The intractability of the road lobby became quite a *cause célèbre*. With the Dornoch bridge, the Wick and Thurso line could have had a viable future as a freight carrier, well placed to take over the traffic when some government finally faces

up to the true cost of road haulage. Without the bridge, the line was doomed to remain meandering, slow and dependent largely on an uncertain tourist business to support the needs of the local population. The decision to keep trains off the Dornoch bridge may well have condemned the whole route to eventual closure.

The result is that the train sets off from Tain to follow the shores of the firth far inland on the first stage of one of those loops that make its route so indirect, and thus so lengthy. These give ample opportunity for the enjoyment of the landscape in considerable leisure, but they make the train travel twice as far as the crow might fly. The reasons are entirely historical.

Work began on the Inverness & Ross-shire Railway in 1860. Its somewhat indirect route northwards, via Dingwall, Invergordon and Tain, was determined both by geography and the whims of local landowners. There were schemes for a more direct route that would cross the Moray, Cromarty and Dornoch firths, but these were opposed by Sir Alexander Mathesson and the Duke of Sutherland, owners of huge estates in the region who felt that they, and Scotland, would benefit from the opening up of the countryside by the inland route. The Duke of Sutherland, a key figure in the line's history, contributed towards its cost on condition that it went via Ardgay, or Bonar Bridge, as the station was then known. The line reached Tain and Bonar Bridge in 1864 and then continued northwards to Lairg. It then turned back towards the coast, to reach the sea at Golspie. This section was built by the Sutherland Railway and completed in 1868. The next section, along the coast from Golspie to Helmsdale, was more extraordinary. In 1870 the Duke of Sutherland obtained approval to build this part of the line, and from then until 1884 passengers were carried along a railway wholly owned and operated by the duke's company. The completion of the line to Wick and Thurso was finally achieved in 1874 by the Sutherland & Caithness Railway, whose equally indirect route inland across isolated moorland avoided difficult terrain. It was also hoped that the railway would open up the country to development, a somewhat fanciful justification

The Duke of Sutherland

One of the richest men in Britain and an influential figure in Victorian life and society, the 3rd Duke of Sutherland was the driving force behind the development of the railway to Wick and Thurso. Indeed, the line was probably unique in being largely the creation of one family. The Sutherland family was known for its interest in contemporary art and industry, on both sides of the border. For many years they enjoyed a particularly fruitful association with Minton, the leading Victorian pottery company, whose Stoke-on-Trent factory was near their English country seat. The duke's largest landholding, however, was in the north of Scotland, and he was keen to develop both agriculture and industry in this region. In the early 1800s the 1st Duke of Sutherland, involved, like so many other Highland lairds in the infamous Clearances, planned herring fisheries at Helmsdale and Golspie to give employment to some of the crofters driven off his estates. It was not until the railway was built, however, that these ports began to flourish. Along with other landowners, the Duke of Sutherland supported the railway from the start, believing it to be the key to the region's economic development.

The duke contributed directly to the line's construction costs and made sure that the route was the one he considered most beneficial. However, his support was more than simply financial, for he took on the responsibility for the construction, and the operating, of the section from Golspie to Helmsdale. From 1870, when construction began, until 1884, when, with the rest of the route, it was taken over by the Highland Railway, the Duke of Sutherland's Railway was one of Britain's most distinctive private lines. He had his own locomotive and rolling stock, and operated a scheduled twice-daily service that became an integrated part of the route once it had reached Wick and Thurso. An enthusiastic railwayman, he was described by one of the navvies employed to build the line as 'a real dook . . . a-driving his own engine on his own railway and a-burning his own blessed coals'.

The line passed close to the Sutherland seat at Dunrobin Castle, where the duke built a private station with an engine shed for his locomotive. Until nationalisation, the dukes of Sutherland retained the right to run a private train on the Wick and Thurso route and to travel to London in their private carriage. Dunrobin station, rebuilt in 1902 in a charmingly eccentric half-timbered style, was fully restored in the 1980s and is still used occasionally for passengers visiting Dunrobin Castle.

Above *The present-day station at Dunrobin, still occasionally used by visitors to the castle*

Below *The opening of the Duke of Sutherland's Railway at Dunrobin in 1870 is graced by the presence of Queen Victoria and the Prince and Princess of Wales*

next station, Lairg, made a major contribution to the line's economy with its famous sheep sales, and for years the railway carried more sheep than people. Now the sheep travel by road, and the trains are emptier than ever.

The route here is particularly attractive, across moorland and through rocky cuttings to its summit, and then along the valley through a landscape of hills broken by old stone walls and dotted with white-painted farms. The train follows the valley down to the sea again, with views of Loch Fleet ahead, and great hills to the north. At The Mound, at the head of Loch Fleet, is the old junction with the former branch to Dornoch. Golspie has quite a grand station, with carved detailing, reflecting its original status as the terminus of the Sutherland Railway. A couple got off here and wandered away into the town's main street, aiming, perhaps, for a few days on the famous sandy beach. The line now follows the route of the former Duke of Sutherland's Railway along the coast, overlooked at the start by the towers of his seat, Dunrobin Castle. Set among woods is Dunrobin station, a delightful half-timbered structure built in 1902, and a pretty folly now used by visitors to the castle. On this occasion there were no visitors and so the train rattled slowly past, its few remaining passengers making the most of the sea views in the evening light. These continued to Brora, a town that once boasted a coal mine, an iron works, mills and some distilleries. There was even an 18th-century wagonway, linking the colliery to the harbour. Later turned into a short industrial line, this survived into this century. It had its own locomotive, a small saddle tank engine built at the Brora ironworks. When Queen Victoria visited the town, she travelled this line, seated in an armchair in an open wagon, hauled by Brora's locomotive.

The seaside journey continues to Helmsdale, along a coastline of lonely, forgotten sandy beaches, with only a golf course to break the isolation. Helmsdale's colour-washed cottages, ranged round the little harbour, have an enjoyable unity. Leaving Helmsdale, the train swings inland, to follow the Helmsdale river on another looping meander into the remote hinterland, empty moorland framed by

Above *The massive bridge at Invershin carries the line high over the Kyle of Sutherland. The bridge links the two stations of Culrain and Invershin, the former serving the popular YHA hostel at Carbisdale Castle*

Opposite *A northbound Sprinter slows down for the speed restriction at Acheilidh level crossing, a small community between Lairg and Rogart*

for what is, in the end, one of Britain's most meandering railway journeys.

After pausing at Ardgay, the train stopped next at the tiny wooden station at Culrain. Here there was a great exodus of people laden with rucksacks who marched off down towards Carbisdale Castle. Originally the home of the Dowager Duchess of Sutherland, for whom the station was opened in 1870, it is now one of the most splendid, and most popular, of Britain's youth hostels. Set above the surrounding woodland, with its mass of towers, the castle is a magnificent sight, and the train provides a grandstand view of it as it crosses the river Shin. For years there was no right of way across the river, and the only way to get to the other side at this point was to take a train from Culrain to Invershin on the northern side.

The train climbed up through the woods, and then out over open moorland, following the river northwards to Lairg, whose cottage-style station is some distance from the little town. Like Rogart, the

big, bare hills, and populated by sheep. Herds of deer may be glimpsed in the distance. From here onwards the journey is steadily more extraordinary, isolated in an empty landscape of subdued colours that merge into a distant horizon, the train pausing at stations so remote that they appear to serve no one. Kildonan stands in the middle of nowhere, while Kinbrace has one or two houses nearby. This region became famous during the building of the line for a small gold rush, when navvies would augment their pay by panning the local rivers, apparently with some success. Even more extraordinarily, at each station some people got off the train, to walk away into the wild and empty landscape, carrying their bags, their guns and their fishing rods. Sometimes other people were on the platform, waiting for the train, with no indication as to how they had got there, or where they had come from. This is a region of shooting lodges and remote country houses, and there is even an occasional hotel hidden in the folds of the hills, no doubt with Range Rovers to deliver visitors to the station – the

practical reality behind the fantasy.

At Forsinard the train passed through the station without stopping, the croft-style building echoing the architecture of a region infamous as a centre of the Highland Clearances, and then the line swings eastwards into what must be one of the most remote stretches of railway in Europe. There were no houses and no roads, just an unchanging landscape of moorland and distant hills, coloured by the lochs, heather and myriad wild flowers. All along the line, snow breaks indicate the harshness of winter, reminders of the annual battle to keep the trains running. At Altnabreac station, an outpost in the middle of nowhere and set among hills that ride the horizon like ships, the young man with the set of antlers left the train, and stood waiting by the track as it pulled away.

Next came Scotscalder, and then, with the landscape softening, there was a distant view of the sea, beyond the Thurso river. At Georgemas Junction, the most northerly in Britain, the train divided, half continuing north to Thurso, and half

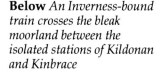

Below *An Inverness-bound train crosses the bleak moorland between the isolated stations of Kildonan and Kinbrace*

Above *Three Highland Railway locomotives in tandem after clearing the line near Wick during the heavy snowstorm of 1909*

Left *Railwaymen brave the freezing weather to inspect a derailed Highland Railway train at Bilbster, between Georgemas Junction and Wick, in the snowstorm of 1909*

Opposite *Wick station in LMS days. Apart from the gas-lighting, little has changed in this shed-like structure*

Below *Proud railway staff pose with their gleaming Highland Railway 4-4-0 No.100 Glenbruar at Wick engine shed, circa 1905*

going eastwards to Wick. This is now a simple process, modern trains having rendered unnecessary complicated manoevring with two locomotives. Some of the magic has, inevitably, been lost. At one time there was also a regular service linking Thurso and Wick, but now passengers have to make their choice, or catch the Dunnet bus.

Descending through farmland, along by the Thurso river, past stone farms with massive stone slab walls, the train drops down to Thurso, and the journey ends in the gaunt sandstone terminus station of 1874, a simple shed-like structure with

timber roof. Wick station is just the same, but built of Caithness flagstone.

The driver stopped his engines, and everyone walked away into the evening light. It was nine-thirty and the short night was still some time away. In Thurso there is a strong sense of being at the top of Britain, and getting there by train gives an intense feeling of well-being. The gulls scream over the harbour, and the clear light patterns the stone buildings. It is a pleasure to be savoured, but it may not last for long, once the accountants get their hands on the most extraordinary train journey in Britain.

The end of the line at Wick.
Highland Railway staff
recorded for posterity for the
camera in 1876